Living in America
Perspectives from an American Chinese

Jason Lin

ISBN: 0692380930
ISBN-13: 978-0692380932 (Linguasoft International Ltd)

DEDICATION

This book is dedicated to my wife Jenny, daughters Sara and Madison for their support in my life and my pursuit of publishing this book.

CONTENTS

ACKNOWLEDGMENTS

I am always grateful to my mother, who passed the gene of language acquisition ability to me. For some reason, when I got accepted into college, majoring in English, my mothers' friends, whom I would call "aunts or uncles" as is the tradition with Chinese culture, somehow thought that my mother taught me English, even though she herself never learned English. I infer that she must have impressed her friends with her ability to learn language. She passed away in 2009, but her influence on me as a child has benefited me tremendously as I grew up to be successful. I thank her for the inspiration she planted in me.

I have been married for more than 30 years. I have to admit that my wife Jenny has a much better sense about literature than I do. In college, while dating her, I tried to read "The Dream of Red Mansion" several times because she had read it several times, but I never completed it. A dozen pages through the novel, I would lose track of the complex web of characters and could not remember the relationship between the characters. Literature is not my cup of tea. My talent is more in language acquisition and study. I am not bored by grammar at all. However, more than 30 years of living with my wife, I have been genetically altered consciously or subconsciously by her talent in literary appreciation. I have developed love for writing due to her influence.

My two daughters Sara and Madison have been the most helpful readers of my writing. They are lovable and part of my life. Without their support, I would not have completed the book.

INTRODUCTION

"Living in America" is a collection of stories or essays I wrote over a span of 25 years. I have told many of the stories to friends at parties or social gatherings many times. Each time I tell my stories, they appreciate the light-hearted way I tell the stories, which are entertaining and often resonate with them in one way or another. After all, they have their own experience that is similar to mine. They have encouraged me to share my stories by publishing them in a book.

I have pondered over the idea of publishing a book for years, but have never mustered enough courage to pursue it. I used to be a young promising scholar in English teaching and research in China. I was a well published researcher before coming to the United States. I was passionate about research. I thought about writing an academic book on American culture or comparison between American culture and Chinese culture. I do have my own insights or perspectives on American culture. I do have something to contribute to the research. However, the idea never came to fruition.

My career took a 180 degrees turn when I came to the United States. As a rising star in the English field in China, I was imbued with confidence in becoming a well-established English scholar after being "gilded" in America. However, I came to America on my own, not on any Chinese government program. I had much more freedom to choose what I would like to do. I was influenced by the mainstream thought of the time that whether you were successful or not depended on whether you were able to get a degree, find a job and settle down in America. For those oversea Chinese students who came to America before the June 4th 1989 Tiananmen Square Incident, the executive order by President Bush provided them with an expedient path to permanent residency or green card. With permanent residency, you have an edge over non-permanent residents in finding a job because your prospective employer does not have to incur the cost and the hassle of sponsoring your work visa, known as H1-B or later green card. However, for those of us, who "missed the boat" and came to America in the early 1990's, the primary and also practical concern was to study in a field that would help enhance the probability of finding a decent job in the future. In other words, a good major was a stepping stone to a bright future. This still holds true today even though it has becoming increasingly hard to find a company willing to sponsor you.

English was hot in China in the 1990's, but no matter how good your English is, you cannot beat a native speaker. Most oversee Chinese view English as a tool, not something you can make a living on. Not that no Chinese pursued English career in America, but that the English related job market for non-native speakers is pathetically limited. It was not uncommon for English majors to switch to Business, Accounting or Computer Science majors. To follow the rule of the survival of the fittest, I had to adapt myself to the challenging reality. With resignation to the concern about my future, I jumped on the bandwagon of switching to business majors and abandoned an otherwise academically promising career. My friends asked me whether I regretted about the decision. Honestly, once in a while, I do get nostalgic about doing research.

On the other hand, switching career from teaching to the business world provided me with a rich and exciting experience. I broke free from the academia of "publish or perish". My job was directly associated with solving business problems. I was able to see how my personal accomplishment directly impacted the business. My impact was more tangible. It was rewarding and gratifying to see how others appreciated my contributions. The transition from academics to business was an adventure that needed courage, but it paid off. Today, as a leader in IT management in a Fortune 100 company, I am very proud of my achievements in the business world.

However, my research DNA has remained active, motivating me now and then to write something. As a habit, I wrote stories and essays when I got inspirations. Looking back at the 25 years of my living in America, I have written dozens of stories and essays on a variety of subjects. These are not research papers. The events or encounters in the book are nothing out of the ordinary. They are not necessarily connected to form a coherent them. However, they represent my perspectives on and feeling about what happened to me. They are neither glamorous nor sensational. Yet it is these seemingly trivial experiences that resonate with people.

Whether you live in America or not, you can appreciate my living experience in America. You may have read American history, American culture, and American politics, but this book presents a unique experience to you. If you are learning English, this book definitely adds to your extensive reading list. I am both excited and happy to share my stories with you. I sincerely hope that you will find them entertaining and resonate with you if you have embarked on a similar journey of pursuing your American dream.

Jason Lin

Cleveland, Ohio, U.S.A

Spring 2015

1 WHERE IS THE UNIVERSITY GATE?

It was right before the breakout of the Gulf War towards the end of 1990. With ups and downs in the process of getting my passport and visa to the United States, I was eventually ready to embark on an overseas study adventure. After 18 hours of flight from Shanghai to Los Angeles, and from Angeles to Pittsburgh, including a couple of hours of waiting time at the LA Airport, I landed at the Pittsburgh Airport in the early morning. The day just broke, but I was not yet fully awake. I had not been able to sleep well, mostly half awake and half asleep during the entire flight. There was not much leg room in the economy class seats. It was the first time I had taken an airplane. All the excitement that had built up prior to the flight soon gave way to the exhausting long journey. Naturally, fatigue overwhelmed me. I looked like a passenger who just got off a red-eyed flight, exhausted and lethargic. I simply wanted to jump on a bed and fall asleep. On the other hand, knowing that I was just 50 miles away from my destination, the Indiana University of Pennsylvania (IUP), I was thrilled about seeing an American university in person. The moment I got my baggage from the claims area, I rushed out to the ground transportation. I need not have rushed. This was America. There was no need to force your way through a crowd to get on a public transportation vehicle such as a bus or a train. Without much trouble, I got on a taxi and headed towards IUP.

The taxi driver was a very friendly middle-aged woman. Her first name was Elizabeth, but she went by Liz, which is a short name for Elizabeth. She knew I was one of those Chinese students who came to the U.S. to study. Each year she picked up dozens of Chinese students from the Pittsburgh Airport and sent them to universities near Pittsburgh. "Welcome to America!" she greeted me with a sweet smile as I stepped into the car. "Thank you!" I replied. The exchange of a few warm words between her and me made me feel at home right away. Americans are well known for their kindness to people. My first encounter with the American lady confirmed my impression.

Since it was in late December, the City of Pittsburgh was enveloped in snow. Snow piled up on both sides of roads. It was obvious that there had been some snow downpours. As the taxi drove out of the airport, going up and down the hilly roads, the white winter landscape caught my eyes. I was fascinated by the wonderful scenery. While in middle school, I read the poem "Qing Yuan Chun--Snow" by the late Chairman of the Chinese Communist Party. I could only imagine the wonder nature bestows to the Northern part of China. Now that I was experiencing the winter beauty of trees dressed in white, I couldn't help but marvel at the northern beauty. I had grown up and lived in the eastern part of China. I had never seen nature clad in snow like this before. If I had a digital camera then, I would have taken as many pictures as I liked, but Kodak films were still expensive. So I selectively took some of the most picturesque scenes with an old traditional camera.

"What a beautiful landscape!" I blurted out, as I clicked, entranced by the snow, covering the land, layered on trees, and sparkling in the sunshine.

"It's typical of here in winter", responded Liz, who saw me fascinated by the snow. "We are simply used to the scene."

A sense of envy for her came across my mind. "Isn't she lucky?" I thought.

The visual satisfaction from the scenery kept me awake all the way. As we continued on our way to IUP, Liz asked questions about me and my family. I asked Liz questions about Pittsburgh and her job as a taxi driver. She was amazed that I could speak English so well. I was curious about everything she had to tell me about America. We chatted and chatted before we realized that we had reached IUP.

"Here you are. This is IUP." Liz pointed at a building about 200 feet away.

As I was paying her the taxi fares, I was perplexed by what I saw. "This place looks nothing like a university", I murmured to myself. "I want to get off at the main gate," I reminded Liz. She stopped her car at the side of a street. There was no gate around. I turned around and saw buildings scattered on a vast expanse of land covered with thick snow. "So, this is the IUP campus?" I questioned Liz with doubt. "Yes, sir!" she answered with a firm tone. Not that I did not trust her, but that I felt I was left on an island with no people around, helpless and lonely. A sense of insecurity struck me, sending a chill down the spine. I shivered more from the fear of the unknown rather than from the cold wind, cutting into my face. I was speechless, but understood that Liz needed to go back to the Pittsburgh Airport. In my judgment, based on my limited interaction with her on the way, she was a trustworthy lady. There was no reason that she would dump me at a strange place and leave me in harm's way. She was too nice and kind to do so. So, I gave her a silk scarf from Suzhou as my gift to her and waved her goodbye. She was very pleased with my gift and wished me good luck as she slowly pulled her car away from me. The only relief I had was that it was about noon time. I still had a few hours to figure out what to do before night fell.

Getting increasingly nervous and concerned, I looked around, hoping to find some people from IUP that could help me out. As I was walking on the campus, scenes of me as freshman being welcomed at the Suzhou Railway station by Suzhou University flashed across my mind. The warmth and the crowd made me feel safe and happy. Now, with cold wind blowing into my face, I was walking on a strange land all by myself! To my disappointment, there was no glamorous structure nearby that looked like something I would call a gate or entrance. I felt deserted or orphaned on an island. A few minutes later, I was excited to see a couple of students walking towards the Sutton Hall, a few hundred feet away from where I stood. It was a historic brick building, similar to brick buildings typically seen on an Ivy League university. "Excuse me!" I shouted at them, waving desperately for help. They heard me and stopped walking. As I approached them, their disarming smile encouraged me to ask them for help. I told them that I was a new foreign graduate student to IUP. I was anxious to find the main entrance to the university. "You are already on the university campus", said one of the students. "There is no main entrance here. The school is closed for the winter break. That's why you do not see many people around." I was still in disbelief that there was no main entrance, but I needed a place to stay for the night. I showed them the brochure sent to me by the International Students Affairs Office. It contained a list of rental properties including dorms and contact information. With their assistance, I was able to find my way to a dorm nearby to settle down for the day. Today, with the Internet and cell phone, it will not be a problem finding a place to live. In those days, however, it was very inconvenient. Landline phones were only available on certain locations. You had to use coins to pay for a call, too.

In China, schools are enclosed with walls or fences. The main gate is the entrance to a school. It is often a symbol of the status of a university. It is often the case that the more magnificent the gate is, the more prestigious the university is. In other words, the gate usually matches the reputation. There is usually an office called "Chuan Da Shi or Message Delivery Room" at the gate. The person manning the gate is probably called "security guard" nowadays. This is where you ask for directions to a building on campus or about a faculty member. It is unimaginable for outsiders to get into a university campus freely, let alone having cars run through the campus. However, here I was, standing on an open campus without a gate. There were no fences or walls surrounding the campus, either. Streets cut through the campus with stop signs at intersections here and there. The open campus is a hallmark of American openness. As a matter of fact, American institutions such as schools and businesses generally do not have fences. It is perhaps one of the first cultural shocks Chinese students will encounter as they start their American adventure.

2 CULTURAL SHOCKS AT IUP CAFETERIA

University cafeterias are popular places where Chinese students work part-time. You get paid at a minimum wage, which was $4.25 in the early 90's. You get free food, too. Like many other Chinese students, I also landed on a cafeteria part-time job, working on the serving line. My job was to stand behind the serving line and pass food to students.

The first day I went to work at the cafeteria of Indiana University of Pennsylvania (IUP), I was filled with curiosity and anxiety. There were two student managers there. Both had blond hair. One went by Nancy and the other by Debbie, which is a short name for Deborah. When dressed in white working polo shirt, both looked similar to me. For the first few days, to my embarrassment, I often confused Nancy with Debbie. Conversely, Nancy and Debbie got confused by some of us Chinese students working there. For some unknown reasons, Americans looked the same to me and we looked the same to them. After a while, I found Nancy and Debbie looked so different and were easily distinguishable by appearance.

Many of us Chinese students used to be scholars teaching at universities. It was a hard feeling to stand behind a serving line passing food to students for several hours. In the western culture, there is a saying that teachers sell their knowledge, priests sell their wisdom and prostitutes sell their bodies. For us scholars to make minimum wages by doing physical work, it is a hard pill to swallow. A sense of dignity loss sometimes hurt me to the marrow. On the other hand, I was not the only Chinese student working at the cafeteria. Many others, who had impressive academic accomplishments in China, worked there, too. For those of us coming to the US in the late 80's, $4.25 an hour was good money. Even if we had scholarships that were adequate for a living, a few hundred extra dollars a month from working at the cafeteria would give us a comfortable financial cushion. To derive fun from working there, we would often joke about "settling down on a foreign land (Yang Cha Dui)" as opposed to "settling down in the countryside (tu cha dui)", which many of us experienced in the mid 70's.

One day, my roommate worked on the salad bar while I served on the serving line. It was a lunch shift. During the peak hour of 11:00 am to 12:00pm, most students would come to eat lunch. The peak hour would keep everybody busy. However, after 12:00pm, things started to slow down. The two student managers Nancy and Debbie were supposed to supervise us student workers. They would walk around and provide assistance as needed. They were also supposed to keep us busy by giving us additional assignments when we were less busy. That's capitalism: maximizing benefits by minimizing costs. I had no problem understanding this capitalist rule. I was happy to do whatever my student manager asked me to do. After all, I was paid to work, not to stay idle. Well, instead of being told to do more work, I would find more work to do if I was not busy. For instance, I would wipe the serving line clean again and again. I would keep the salad bar clean by cleaning it every few minutes. Americans describe this type of workers as self-motivated. You do not need to tell them to perform. They are motivated to perform well. My hard work paid off. The two student managers would give me more hours to work. They called me "the salad bar man" because I kept the salad bar clean all the time.

My roommate Yu also liked to work on the salad bar because it was a relatively easy job. How hard would it be to replenish ingredients on a salad bar? Doing the dishes in the hot dish room was much more demanding physically. One day, Yu worked on the lunch shift manning the salad bar. Being very talkative person, he derived great satisfaction from interactive conversations with people. He did a nice job greeting customers, who were mostly American students with a meal plan. As things started to slow down, he was bored standing by the bar, a little bit restless. After being idle for a while, he walked to a nearby table where a few Chinese students were done eating but still sitting there, talking and joking. They talked and talked, laughter bursting out now and then. It was certainly a lot easier to kill time that way. Yu could not resist his inner desire to join the conversation. Gesticulating wildly, he got carried away while telling a Chinese joke. All of a sudden, he saw the cafeteria manager Jack right by him. The laughter must have caught Jack's attention. "You are not supposed to be talking while on salad bar duty." Jack reminded Yu politely. Feeling embarrassed, Yu got defensive and refused to say sorry. He looked humiliated by Jack's remark in front of others. "I'm not a machine!" he rebuked, meaning human beings need to talk. The response caught Jack by surprise. Jack was a seasoned professional manager. He was well trained in handling employees. He was not prepared to handle a Chinese student worker, who directly confronted him with a strong statement about human beings' need to talk. He was torn between laughing and crying (ku xiao bu de). He shook his head and walked away. He did not want to engage in a quarrel with a student worker.

Indeed, human beings need to talk at work place. However, there is no justification for leaving your job and engaging in a non-work related chat. Jack got a cultural shock himself. It was not simply a matter of insubordination by employees. Yu failed to understand performing work the American way. The American work ethic sets expectation that employees will not abuse work time. Work is work.

Yu later admitted that he was wrong. He behaved emotionally and irrationally in the situation. His response to Jack was not acceptable. He thought he would be fired the next day, but to his pleasant surprise, Jack only moved him to the dish room, depriving him of the privilege to work on the salad bar. In America, do not defend your mistake before your boss unless you are innocent. Admission is the best policy if you do make a mistake.

As coincidence would have it, a week later, Jack encountered another cultural shock. Another Chinese student by the name of Liu was assigned to clean tables, a job similar to that of a bus boy at restaurants. Again, as things slowed down, there were not many tables to clean. So Liu walked around, briefly stopping to talk to acquaintances. The manager gesticulated for Liu to come over by bending his fingers towards himself, a provoking gesture commonly seen in a Chinese Kong Fu movie scene where one person invites another to a fight. Liu was mad at the gesture. Feeling insulted, he walked to Jack and burst into rage. "Don't do that to me again!" he threatened with a fiery expression. Jack stood there speechless. A few students, some American and some Chinese, were appalled by the scene. When I heard Liu's angry voice, I went to him to chill him down. I explained to Jack that it was misunderstanding due to cultural differences. Liu was generally a friendly guy. I had never thought he would behave rudely like that. I could hardly believe the incident if I had not seen it in person.

Poor Jack! He probably would never have anticipated being culturally shocked twice in a couple of weeks. What went through his mind? Did he think Chinese students were weird and rude? Instead of us Chinese students experiencing American cultural shocks, we brought cultural shocks to Jack.

One of the benefits of working at the cafeteria was that you could eat as much as you could. The abundance of food at the cafeteria was impressive. It showed that America is a rich country, where food is not rationed and plentiful. Well, Chinese students, as international students, only work or rather are only allowed to work part-time at the cafeteria. To save cooking time, some students would take leftover food home after work.

One day, Lu, a Ph. D student in Chemistry, worked on the serving line until the cafeteria closed. He could not resist the temptation to take some leftover chicken legs home. He carefully wrapped the legs in a piece of foil and dropped it in his backpack. The student manager on duty caught him right in the act. "Mr. Lu, throw the chicken legs into the dish room. No food shall be taken out of here!" the student manager insisted.

Embarrassed and blushed, Lu rebutted "These are leftovers. What a waste to throw them away!"

"You must follow the rule. Period!" The student manager emphasized.

With hesitation, Lu did what he was told to. Indeed, for us Chinese students who had not seen such abundance of food, it was hard to understand why Americans would waste so much food. It is not uncommon to eat leftovers at home. What's the big deal with taking home leftovers from the cafeteria? It took a while for us Chinese students to get over this cultural shock. Later, we learned that American businesses would rather avoid liability than do what seems to be reasonable. It sounds reasonable for people to take leftovers home because they will be thrown away after all. However, if anyone gets sick or is poisoned by the leftover food, the liability could be placed on the business that allows the leftover to be taken home. No business wants to be involved in lawsuits of this kind.

3 IGNORANCE ABOUT AIDS

I started my journey of overseas study at Indiana University of Pennsylvania (IUP) at the end of 1990. While there was so much to absorb in a foreign culture, I was very sensitive to topics related to AIDS (Acquired Immunodeficiency Syndrome). The reason was that in the late 80's and early 90's, HIV (Human Immunodeficiency Virus) was a big scare to the public. Everybody knew that there was no cure for AIDS, a disease that HIV carriers would eventually develop. Mere mention of AIDS could send chill down your spine. It was a hot topic on American campuses then.

 One day, on the way to school, I overheard students talking about Magic Johnson, a NBA super star, who disclosed to public that he had been diagnosed as HIV positive. Being a professional basketball player, Magic Johnson looked strong and perfectly healthy. There was no symptom signaling he was HIV positive. Isn't it scary to interact with somebody who is a HIV carrier but looks normal? The more I thought about it, the more scared I became when passing other students on the hallway or sitting next to an American student. If I saw someone looking sick or feeble, I would try to stay away from that person for fear of catching HIV. When someone coughed or sneezed close to me, it could deprive me of a peaceful night. Ignorance leads to stupid behavior. My fear of HIV was a case in point.

However, I was not the only person with ignorance about AIDS. At the dorm I stayed, approximately 20% of the tenants were Chinese students. The dorm was a four-story apartment building with shared showers and toilets. The AIDS topic would pop up among the Chinese students relatively frequently. Who would not be scared of contracting AIDS? One of the concerns was sharing toilets with American students. Many Chinese students at that time believed that direct skin contact could cause HIV infection. They thought that, like TB, HIV could be airborne or via touch. A shared toilet obviously was perceived to be the most dangerous place to get HIV infection. There is no way to tell whether the previous person sitting on the toilet carries HIV or not. When a person shows symptoms of AIDS, it is already too late. To be on the safe side, one of the Chinese girls on the fourth floor shared her smart prevention method with other Chinese girls in the dorm. She would pull long strips of toilet paper and lay them around the toilet seat so that her skin would not have direct contact with the seat rim. The landlord was mad to see lots of toilet paper dropped on the restroom floor. The landlord threatened to fine whoever wasting toilet paper that way. In spite of a warning notice posted on the wall to the effect that do not drop toilet paper on the floor, the need to prevent AIDS obviously overweighed the need to abide by the rule. After all, one's health is more important. Who would want to risk of getting infected with HIV? However, nobody wanted to be fined, either. So, some Chinese girl came up with a creative, but disrespectful idea—pee the man's style.

Instead of sitting on the seat and answering the nature's call, a couple of Chinese girls would stand and pee the man's style. As a result, spills of urine over the toilet rim were inevitable. To make the matter worse, those girls would not clean the spills. They would leave the cleaning job to the cleaning lady, who would clean the restroom only once a day. Some American girls were already annoyed by strips of toilet paper on the floor. It was wasteful and disgusting. Peeing the man's style, however, turned out to be the last straw to the American girls. They could not put up with it any more. One of the American girls got so mad that she posted a sign in the restroom, saying "Go back to China and pee in your own country!"

The sign naturally humiliated the Chinese girls on the fourth floor. It was perceived to be an indication of prejudice against Chinese students. They showed strong solidarity in protesting against this kind of prejudice. They could not tolerate the American girl's behavior. "If we remain silent on this matter, they can poop on our heads. We must do something about it," one of the Chinese girls tried to stir up the emotion of the others. "Yes!" others concurred. After ventilating their anger, they decided to lodge a formal written complaint to the president of IUP. The president treated the matter seriously and promptly. He directed the provost to handle the matter on his behalf. The provost investigated the matter and facilitated a conversation between the two parties involved. The American girl who had posted the sign explained that her behavior was simply her way of ventilating her anger at the inappropriate way of peeing by the Chinese girls. She was by no means biased against the Chinese students involved in the incident. She apologized for having unintentionally hurt them. The Chinese girls accepted her apology and also returned their own apology for not using the toilet the proper way. Both sides agreed that the incident was due to misunderstanding.

After the incident, the university health services distributed educational materials on AIDS to foreign students. We learned that skin contact would not spread HIV from person to person. The common cause is through blood transmission or needle sharing. It is safe to use publicly shared toilets. Beneath the seemingly funny story is a dark truth: human ignorance leads to stupidity. Whether it is in America or in China, we human beings make stupid mistakes because of our own ignorance.

4 DO NOT LEAVE YOUR CHILD ALONE AT HOME

As planned, I took my wife Jenny out to practice driving on Saturday. Her road test was scheduled for the following Monday day. She failed the first test the week before. In Ohio, the road test has two parts: driving test and maneuverability test. Jenny passed the driving test without a glitch. However, she was very upset because she was so close to finish the maneuverability test when her car hit a cone. Well, a miss is as good as a mile. Even if she barely hit the cone, she failed the entire test. What a pity! She wanted to pass the test as soon as possible so that she could drive by herself.

In America, if you do not speak English, you cannot communicate with others. If you cannot drive, you cannot move around. The public transportation system may not be a problem if you live in a major city such as New York and Chicago. In suburban areas such as Kent, Ohio, where we lived, having a car is a necessity. Moreover, my wife was baby-sitting a friend's daughter. I had to drive her to and from the friend's house. It was a big inconvenience. Anxious to pass the road test, she got up early in the morning and urged me to go as soon as we finished breakfast.

Our daughter was then a third grader. She was still in bed, sleeping like a log. After all, it was a Saturday. She deserved a good rest after a busy school week plus intensive after-school activities. Not to wake her up, we left a note at the night stand next to her bed. "Dad and Mom will be back in a couple of hours", the note said. She knew what to eat for breakfast: cereal plus milk. She was old enough to take care of herself, so we left her alone at the apartment we rented. It was a big apartment complex with many two-storied apartment buildings. Students who lived there were mostly graduate students with families. It was a popular place for Chinese students because the price was reasonable. It was close to the main campus. We lived on the second floor of Building A. Our apartment had a large bedroom, a small one and a living room sharing the space with the kitchen. Each apartment had a bathroom with a shower and bath tub. The apartment was cozy and big enough for the family of three. In fact, it was even better than the one we in Suzhou, China.

It was late April. Warm and breezy, it was a perfect day for outing. Cherry trees were blossoming everywhere. Blue jays and cardinals were flying happily from tree to tree, chirping and twittering. As we drove to the parking lot at the Kent State football stadium, we were in pretty good mood. The parking lot was empty with nobody else, as if we temporarily owned the parking lot for our exclusive usage. There is no better place for practicing maneuverability than a large parking lot. It is always a challenge coaching your spouse on anything! What matters is not so much in whether you give right instructions as in how she feels about your instructions. Since her goal was to pass the maneuverability test as soon as possible, she followed my instructions respectfully most of the time. The maneuverability drill repeated again and again until Jenny felt ready for a second test. She was so focused on the practice that it was lunch time before we realized it. Filled with confidence, we drove back to the apartment with a sense of accomplishment, which, together with the gorgeous weather, kept us in happy mood.

Approaching the parking lot behind our apartment, we spotted two police cars parked at the parking lot, with their blue and red lights flashing.

"What's going on?" my wife asked.

"I don't know" I replied. "Someone must be in trouble," I suspected.

As we got into the parking lot, I suddenly had a hunch that we were in trouble. Something could have happened to our daughter. I left no time getting off the car and rushed upstairs to our apartment.

"Are you Mr. Lin?" questioned a police officer.

"Yes, sir" I answered, with a shivering voice. "What happened?"

Our daughter was standing in the kitchen in her pajamas. She clearly looked scared and bewildered. She had cried for a while.

"You have endangered your child. Do you understand that?" the police officer explained to me.

16

"Hmm..., but how?" I still did not understand what I had done wrong.

"You left your daughter alone at home. You have endangered her. She was taking a shower when the smoke detector sounded like crazy. Your next door neighbor called 911 about the situation. Luckily, your daughter was fine." The police officer offered some details about what had happened.

"Well, she's just taking a shower. How could that be endangering her life?" I argued, still thinking the police officer made a mountain out of a mole.

"What if she trips in the bath tub and gets hurt? Child endangerment is against Ohio law. You can be put in prison if your child is hurt." The police officer's voice sounded more serious.

"I'm terribly sorry!" I apologized to the officer, realizing that I was in trouble. "In China, we often do that. This incident was due to our lack of understanding of American law. Please pardon us." I tried to explain this off.

The moment I uttered the excuse I regretted it. After all, in America, ignorance is no defense. You cannot break a law because you do not know about the law. The more you try to find an excuse, the worse it becomes. Admission of the wrong doing is the best policy. I realized that any defense would come to no avail. So I admitted to the officer that I was wrong to leave my daughter alone at home and asked for forgiveness.

"Come over here" the police officer pointed to the stove. "Luckily, nothing was cooking on the stove while you were out. Otherwise, it would have been a more serious offense. What if something burns and causes a fire? You know what I mean?"

"We made sure we turned off everything before we left." At least we had a sense of safety. If we had left something cooking, a fire accident could have occurred, although it was a chance in a million. "I will make sure we never do this again." I sounded guilty of the child endangerment act, hoping my good attitudes would make a difference to the officer's decision on the case.

I was impressed by the officer's professionalism. He did nothing inappropriate in handling the case. He filled the case report and asked me to sign it. From his attitudes, I sensed that we would be fine. He would not bring child endangerment charges against us. I could not image my wife and me appearing in court. The shame would be too much to bear. Thanks God! Our innocent mistake did not cause any disaster.

I thought the case was over. The agonizing moments finally came to an end. What a relief!

"You and your wife are required to go through the Child Endangerment Training Program. A social worker will contact you for an appointment next week. You must complete the training program within 30 days," The police officer told us.

At first I couldn't believe my ears. I thought it was over, but not knowing what it was like to go through the program made me very nervous. Was it something like correction center? I hoped not.

"What is it? Do we have to?" I asked innocently, hoping we could be spared the inconvenience.

"It's a training program. You will get education about child endangerment law. It's not optional." The police officer sounded firm, suggesting that it was not a matter for negotiation.

"Okay, Okay!" I promised to the officer. "We will complete the training as required." After all, the outcome of this incident was much better than expected.

After the police officer left, I could not wait to hear my daughter's story. She had not completely recovered from the scary experience yet. With tears in her eyes, she recounted what had happened. She forgot to close the bathroom door before taking shower. The steam kept flowing out of the bathroom, triggering the smoke detector. She was scared to death. She was helpless. She had no clue what to do. All she did was crying. My heart broke as she told her story tearfully. I would never do this again!

I learned a big lesson from this. I shared the story with Chinese friends at gatherings. America is a law-abiding society. Ignorance is no defense! To survive in America, we need to change our mindset about living in America. What works in China may not work in America. Do as Americans do.

5 STOP YELLING AT ME, MOM!

The 2012 Annual Cleveland Chinese Tennis Tournament was held again during the Labor Day weekend. A few dozen players, old and young, men and women, boys and girls, gathered to compete for the championship titles for men's single, boys' single (16 and under), girls' single (16 and under), and double, which had no age restriction. My daughter Madison, who had taken private tennis lessons for a year, was excited to attend the event. Being eleven years' old, she was the youngest of all. In sports, especially in America, participation is more important than winning. Win or lose, it is a good experience. That's how you grow. Fair competition helps develop your sportsmanship.

Madison played hard in her first match. She beat a girl who was 4 years older in a close game. Both Madison and her opponent tried their best. I was pleased with the athleticism and efforts Madison exhibited during the match. I could not be more proud of Madison for her accomplishment. While I was commending Madison for her excellent performance, I overheard another girl shouting back at her mom. "Stop yelling at me, Mom! You're not being helpful! " The girl's mom was criticizing her daughter for not winning the game against her opponent. I felt bad about the girl. Yelling was a distraction rather than help to the girl. The girl ended up losing the match. The girl's mom obviously hurt her daughter's pride and embarrassed her in public. The sharp exchange between the mom and the daughter made me think about the difference between Chinese parents and American parents.

I have never heard an American parent blaming a child for not winning a game. "It's alright, Luke. You were doing great!" is a popular comment an American parent might make about the loss of a game. American parents feel proud about their children for participating in the game and working hard to win. They are the best and most devoted spectators for their children whether it is a home game or an away game. Chinese parents, on the other hand, have the game result written on their facial expressions. If both Chinese parents and American parents go to a game, you can tell the result by looking at the facial expression of a Chinese parent. We Chinese parents care too much about the result rather than the journey to the result.

American parents are more encouraging and positive towards their children. What is "so-so" to us Chinese parents may be "great" to American parents. Of course, "so-so" and "great" are relative terms. Chinese parents generally put more pressure on their children. No matter what their children do, Chinese parents set a high bar, often with unrealistic expectations. They know not every Chinese piano student can be a top pianist like Long Long. They know not every Chinese tennis player can be Mike Chang. In practice, however, they just do the opposite, pushing their children as far as they can. They are more like "tigers" than "pandas". Their children, who grow up in America, where positive comments are expected, find themselves in a cultural conflict. At school, they may be praised by their teachers for projects. At private music lessons, they may be commended for great performance. At sports drill, they may be viewed as "future stars" by their coaches. In short, they live in a positive culture and feel good about themselves. However, their experience with their parents is a different story. At home, their parents may demand more than expected by school teachers because they have high hopes for their children, who are, so to speak, "dragons in the making" to the minds of their parents. Extra homework, extra piano practice time, and extra sports practice time are common complaints from Chinese children. Home is more like a pressure cooker while school is more like a fun park.

I raised the first daughter the Chinese way. Like other Chinese parents, I belonged to the tiger family. I was probably a fierce tiger to her. I was too demanding. My attention was focused much more on her achievements than the journey to success. As she grew older, she became more and more rebellious to me. Our relationship was strained increasingly because she failed to live up to my high expectations. She simply would turn a deaf ear to my coaching, or at times, admonition. She would lock herself up in her room to avoid my lecturing on the importance of working harder to achieve more. The communication channel between us was virtually shut down. Her memory of childhood spent with me was mostly unpleasant, deprived of fun, which children would like to have. If I could relive the past, I would rather be a panda dad than a tiger dad. To a child, nothing can compensate for the loss of fun memory. I wish I had been a role model for her and had encouraged and motivated her to achieve more in her life instead of pushing her hard.

As luck would have it, God blessed my family with a second daughter, Madison, who is fifteen and half years apart from her big sister. My constant exposure to American way of educating children has helped me to rethink about my way of raising children. The pain and frustration I brought to my first daughter during her growth are not to be repeated. I am determined to raise Madison not the tiger way. I have been much more sensitive to Madison's feeling. I would stay positive about anything that has happened to her. When she brings home her tests, I will genuinely show my pride and praise her generously. When she makes a mistake, I will sympathize with her and share with her my perspective on the mistake from a positive angle. During her tennis practice, I will say "Great job!" to her if she makes a good shot. When she gets tired and starts to slack off, I will say "Come on, Madison, you can do it!" Instead of pushing Madison, I have made all my efforts to inspire her and motivate her. She has done a fantastic job both at academic work and extracurricular activity such as music and sports. I cannot be more proud of her. Although I occasionally show the characteristics of a "tiger", I have managed to minimize the occurrence of tiger behavior on my part. If I do lose temper, possibly due to my "tiger" DNA, I will do my best to offset the negative impact with love and care for Madison. I want to leave a positive and happy childhood memory with Madison. Seeing her grow with happiness gives me great relief. Seeing her adorable smile makes me smile. Her happiness infuses me with happiness. A fearful and harsh dad to the first daughter has been transformed into a reasonable and more encouraging dad to the second one!

What is lost cannot be regained. Let our children enjoy their childhood more. Let's not yell at them for faltering or progressing slower than expected. All children deserve a happy childhood. Every single step our child takes is a step forward to becoming a mature adult. As parents, we can help our children grow by leading them rather than pushing them, by understanding them rather blaming them, and by encouraging them rather than pressurizing them. If we maintain a positive attitude, our world may look positive to us. A positive parent is more likely to unleash his or her child's dream about the bright future. A child, who dreams big, is more likely to be motivated to work persistently towards a set goal. On the contrary, a pressure cooker will crush a child's dream and destroy the child's potentials for success.

6 CAN I HAVE A DOLLAR?

On a summer night, I was walking across a parking lot to my apartment. I had studied for several hours in the university library for the final exam. My brain was exhausted, but the air was refreshing, so I tried to breathe as much air as I could. My mind was still preoccupied with the questions on the study guide. All of a sudden, I saw a tall guy approaching me. The parking lot did not have good lighting. I could see the shadow moving towards me. I was freaking out, thinking he was going to rob me. I did not see anybody else nearby. I did not have money with me. I wish I had some, at least a few dollars. I remembered the advice my friend, who spent a year in New York, offered me at a farewell party for my overseas adventure: Keep a few dollars with you when you go out. If a bad guy asks you for money at a bus stop or on the street, give him the money. If you don't, he may hurt you. I was in Indiana, Pennsylvania. It was a rural town. It was a relatively safe place. Maybe, I just had bad luck, I thought. I was getting increasingly nervous as the man got within 20 feet of me. I dared not run because I was afraid that he might shoot me. In fact, even if I wanted to run, I would not be able to because my legs would not take orders from my brain any more. I simply stood where I was, motionless and hopeless.

"Can I have a dollar?" the man asked me without sounding menacing.

I heard his request clearly, but did not utter a sound, shivering hard.

"Do you have a dollar?" the man tried again, looking at me with suspicion. His eyes showed no menacing signs of hurting me.

I pretended not to understand him, looking like a prey yielding to the hunter. Looking at me up and down, the man uttered some f-words and walked away without harming me. I rushed to the apartment, relieved. I told the story to my friends.

"Don't worry. That tall guy is a homeless person. He often hangs around on the parking lot and asks foreign students for money," one of them said.

"Did you give him any money?" asked another. "No," I replied. "I did not have any money with me at that time."

"Next time you'd better carry some money with you," my roommate advised me. "Some bad guys may hurt you if they do not get anything from you".

I wondered why the guy let me go without harming me. Perhaps he just wanted to get some money. He never intended to harm an innocent person like me. Or maybe he thought I did not understand his English because I remained silent. Whatever the reason, it was inconceivable to me at that time that I could encounter homeless people in person. I never heard beggars in American before, let alone homeless people. My image of America as paradise was then tarnished. Later, I learned that homeless people are one of the main social problems in America.

In China, I used to see beggars knocking at your door for food because a natural disaster such as flood destroyed crops. The affected peasants would go begging for survival. In America, however, I have never seen beggars on the street. How come there are homeless people?

In America, homelessness is attributable to a variety of factors. Homelessness is first and foremost an economic problem. A number of social and political factors also contribute to the problem. The number of people experiencing homelessness exploded in the 1980s, as federal funds were withdrawn from low-income housing and social assistance programs for low-income families and the mentally ill. Current federal spending on housing assistance programs targeted at low-income populations is less than 50% of 1976 spending levels.

Economically, lack of affordable housing is a major factor. As rich as America is to the outside world, millions of American families and individuals are not able to make ends meet. This is because the gap between wage earnings and the cost of housing in the United States has been growing steadily for the past decades. According to the National Low Income Housing Coalition, families across America would need to earn a "housing wage" of $15.37 an hour, nearly three times the current minimum wage, to afford a two-bedroom apartment at the average fair market rent.

Not surprisingly, many low and minimum wage workers cannot afford food and shelter. Over the past twenty-five years, wages for the lowest income workers have not kept pace with the increase in living costs. The minimum wage has continually decreased in value since the late 1960s; adjusting for inflation, the current minimum wage is worth 27% less than it was in 1968. As a result, the lowest income workers can hardly afford necessities such as housing and food.

The cost of health care and insurance has rocketed dramatically over past years. Health care can cost a family up to $8000/year. For families living on low or middle incomes, this cost can be prohibitive. As Chinese often say, "Good health means happiness to the poor." But as luck would have it, the poor cannot necessarily maintain a healthy life style. For families or individuals that lack health insurance, a sudden illness, chronic disease, or accident can be financially devastating.

Politically, cuts in federal assistance for housing programs and social services have coincided with the rise in homelessness in the U.S. The 1950s and 1960s witnessed near eradication of homelessness through federal housing programs and services; however, during the 1980s, housing programs were slashed by half and the homeless population in the U.S. began to grow.

While economic factors are the main causes of homelessness, long-term issues like mental illness, drug addiction, and alcoholism can exacerbate situations of poverty and put people at greater risk of homelessness. Surveys of people experiencing homelessness show that about 25% of the homeless population suffers from some form of mental illness; the high cost of health insurance leaves homeless people without access to proper care to treat mental illness. Drug and alcohol addiction affect about 20% of the homeless population who, again, often lack access to proper, affordable care for these illnesses.

In the past 25 years, I have seen homeless people in many places, especially in cities. Some carry their belongings in a shopping cart and live a mobile life. Others find shelter under bridges. Still others sleep on heat ventilation openings on streets in winter so that they will not be frozen to death. Each time I spot a homeless person, the first encounter I had with a homeless person many years ago will come back to me vividly. I can hear him ask me the question again and again. "Can I have a dollar?"

7 CAN I HAVE 5 BUCKS FOR BEER?

It was the Black Friday after the Thanksgiving holiday. There had not been much snow throughout the winter, but the Black Friday witnessed one of the heaviest snow storms in the history of the Northeast Ohio area. I had just returned from Chicago the night before. I was still in the fast driving mode because on the way back from Chicago, the weather was nice. The speed limit on Interstate 80 is 70 miles. Typically drivers add about 10 miles to the limit without a problem. It is an understood rule between drivers and highway patrol cops. Since it had not snowed much, my driving skill for the slippery road got a bit rusty. I kept reminding myself to drive slowly and cautiously. But I was going at 60 miles per hour on the Interstate 480, which was the highway I would take to work. The visibility was not great, but my right foot stayed on the gas pedal to maintain the speed.

As I was getting off 480 at the Bedford exit, all of a sudden I saw cars lined up on the ramp, which was curving with a slope. I stepped on the brake right away, but my car, which was not a 4-wheel drive sedan, skidded, and the car continued to spin until the back hit the back of a utility van. "Bang," The moment I heard the noise, I could feel the impact. I got off the car and was upset to see the back bumper of my car hanging down, almost touching the road. The driver of the utility van got out. He was a skinny, young man. I approached his car and inspected the back door, which my bumper hit. There was a barely noticeable dent. His van had metal back doors. No wonder it was only a very light dent even though my back bumper was completely ruined.

"Can we settle this between us?" I asked him, thinking it was my fault, and if he reported the case to the police, my insurance premium would go up. Plus, I had an important meeting to attend in the morning. I would like to take a detour and leave the scene as soon as possible.

He was still checking the van patiently. "How about," I followed up with my honest offer. "100 dollars in cash?"

"No. It's not my van. It's the company's van," he declined with a reasonable explanation. He sounded like an honest guy with no intention to rip me off. I appreciated his honesty.

"But there's really no noticeable damage to the van," I insisted, trying to close the deal. "Look, my back bumper is badly damaged. It will cost me a fortune to fix it. You know, body repair is not cheap." I sounded as if I was pleading with him for a private deal.

"Sorry," he countered. "But I can't cut the deal with you. I want to report the case."

It was such a bad day that there were several collision accidents ahead of us on the same ramp. We waited and waited but no police officer showed up in half an hour.

"Are you sure you want to wait further?" I said to him. "Looks like there are too many accidents for the police to handle today."

"I know, but I would like to wait," he insisted again, showing no sign of impatience.

I could not but wait impatiently. I knew I was going to miss the meeting. So I called my boss and let him know what had happened. My boss sympathized with me and told me not to worry about the meeting. So I stayed in the cold, waiting and waiting. Another half an hour passed when a police officer showed up on a motor cycle.

"What's the matter?" he asked, seeing the damaged bumper hanging at the back of my car.

"He hit my van," the man told the police officer.

"It's a minor case," said the officer, as if nothing had happened. After all no one had been hurt. "There are so many cases today. Are you still able to drive your car?" The officer directed his question to me.

"Yes, sir," I replied, knowing my fate was now in his hands.

"Here is the address," the officer handed a slip with the address of the Bedford Police Station. "Go there by yourselves and they will take care of the case for you."

So, we both turned around and I followed him all the way to the Bedford Police Station.

Not surprisingly, there was a long line inside the station. I assumed that these people were all involved in a minor accident so they could drive here as we did. I was already mentally prepared to take the day off as I had no idea how long it would take to complete the case filing.

The longer I waited, the more I thought about the man. Why would he not cut a deal with me? He could have just taken 100 dollars and go back to his business. Was this because he was a person of integrity and would not want to bend any rules? Or was this because he had a strong sense of code of ethics and was simply following his company's policy? From the picture on his van, I could tell he worked for a plumbing business. There are many small businesses in America that provide plumbing, air conditioning and heat services to local communities. So I started to form a positive impression about the man.

He was a smoker. An hour and half waiting in the line was more than he could bear. He went outside and lit up a cigarette. As smoke whiffing into the air, he got a call. I guessed that it must have been his boss. A few minutes later, he came back inside and said to me, "Can I have 5 bucks for a beer?"

"What do you mean?" I did not quite understand why he asked money for a beer.

"If you give me 5 bucks, I will not file the case and the matter will be settled," he explained, sounding like he was offering me an attractive deal.

"Are you sure?" I wanted to confirm.

"Yes. I have to go to a customer right now."

I couldn't be happier to hear that. I took out my wallet and grabbed a five dollar bill.

"Here you go," I handed the money to him.

"Thank you!" he smiled and left in a hurry.

We pretty much wasted 3 hours waiting. I was upset. It was almost noon by the time he left. I was no longer in the mood for work that day. I was not sure whether I could get to work given so many accidents on the road. So I decided to head home instead.

On the way home, I thought about the young man. What positive impression I had about him had been gone by now. If he had been an honest person of integrity, he should not have asked me for 5 bucks. On the other hand, if he had been a greedy, selfish guy, he could have taken my initial offer of 100 dollars. I could not read his mind. It beat me the way he had behaved. It was totally beyond my comprehension. What had started out as a stressful event ended in a hilarious manner. If he had asked me for 100 dollars as originally offered, I would have probably honored his request. After all, my goal was to settle the case privately so that I would not have to incur the increased on-going car insurance premium. As luck would have it, it only cost me 5 bucks to settle the case.

8 CAMPING – MY FIRST OUTDOOR ADVENTURE

I am not an outdoor person. I seldom, if not never, do hiking in the woods. I do not find fun in fishing. To me nothing wears on your mind more than impatient waiting for a fish to bite your bait. It is no surprise camping is never top on my list of options for vacation. I simply enjoy competitive indoor sports such as ping pong and badminton.

Sometimes I wonder why some people would like to go camping away from their comfortable home. I have a neighbor who often goes camping on weekends. He and his family are such passionate campers that they literally go camping all year around even when the weather is not cooperative. He has an RV (recreational vehicle). Often on Fridays, I see his family busy packing stuff for camping for weekends. They must be true camping lovers. Why would you sleep in a RV, which is no comparison in comfort with your cozy home? I don't get it!

This year, as summer was drawing to a close, my friends suggested that we go out camping at the West Branch, a popular camping site located in Northeastern Ohio. Magically, we were able to reserve a couple of camping sites for five families. The same families except mine went to the same place two years ago, but their stay there was ruined by a heavy rain downpour. The weather forecast was not encouraging. It would be wet through the weekend of our planned stay. The unpleasant memory from the other families, and the ominous weather would have deterred me from going. For some reason, there was an urge from my heart to embark on this adventure. My default response to camping has been "not me". This time, however, I was excited about the trip. I just wanted to experience it and feel what it was like sleeping in the open.

Since I had never done camping before, I had to get all the camping equipment. The good news is that camping preparation is a no brainer today. You can get everything you need from a major retailer such as Wal-Mart. You can find tents that can be set up in minutes. Most tents have a tub floor to prevent rain from getting to your sleeping bag. Depending on the number of campers, you can even get a tent with two bedrooms and one living room. The living area is the size of a decent one bedroom apartment. You can choose a sleeping bag that makes sleeping comfortable under a specified temperature range such as 40-60 degrees Fahrenheit.

Typically, camping sites have bathroom for showers. There are power outlets for using electricity. You can grill hot dogs, hamburgers, corns or whatever you like on grills. Bonfires are one of the best things kids and adults both like. Camp sites are near water. Campers can canoe in the river or enjoy a boat ride in the lake. For those fishing fans, catching a fresh fish and adding it to your dinner is exciting. Camp sites are well organized like housing communities. Each site has a number. You can only set up your tent at a lot assigned to you.

With everything ready, we set out to the camping site late Friday afternoon. Twenty years ago, everywhere we went, we would get a map from a Triple A agency to study the route carefully. With the Internet mapping service available, you can print out the driving directions easily from Yahoo maps or Google maps. Today, GPS device is common. So, all we needed to do was enter the destination address and let the GPS device tell us the direction. As luck would have it, a road leading to the camp site was blocked for repair. There was no clear detour sign. We arrived really late at the site after taking an alternative route. While driving through the camping site to find our lot, I was amazed that the site boasted a couple of hundred lots. The entire site was full for the weekend. There must have been more than a thousand camp lovers gathered there for the weekend. Colorful tents with different shapes and sizes were set up neatly. Just like houses are built on both sides of streets, camping lots are also along both sides of roads. Many campers brought their RVs, parked in an orderly fashion. People in groups were riding bikes. Camp lights were scattered like stars. All this contributed to a marvelous view of the tent community. The whole site looks like a housing community except that tents and RVs are lined up along roads instead of houses. People did not know each other, but they were friendly and sociable.

As night fell, all kids went into the tents playing their own games. We adults sat around the bonfire, chatting about life, work or whatever random topics that would pop up. It was quite relaxing and romantic. All the stress from work was completely off my mind. As the sky got darker, stars appeared.

God really blessed us. Instead of rain, we saw countless stars glittering in the sky. Gazing at the stars gave me a special feeling I never had before. It was truly romantic to gaze at the twinkling stars with your significant other next to you. It was so tranquil and peaceful. Each star seemed to be telling us a touching story about the galaxy.

We chatted and chatted until we burned all the fire woods bought for the day. It's time to go to bed so that we could have energy for the following day. It started to get windy around midnight. The wind was blowing hard now and then, as if lifting up the tent and we would fly away. At times, I was a bit scared. But my daughter slept like a log. The sky cleared up in the early morning. We woke up fresh. All through the night I could smell the freshness in the air. The feeling was absolutely cool!

After a simple breakfast, we all went on a hiking trip along the lake shore and through the woods. It was amazing to see so many huge trees fallen on the ground. Trees come and go, but the woods continue to exist. That's the cycle of life. Some huge trees were clearly struck down by thunder. From the decaying tree trunks grew some exotic colorful mushrooms. They looked so beautiful, but we had to resist our temptation to eat them. Nobody knew they were poisonous or not. As we were crossing a stream, we saw a giant tree lying across the stream, creating a single log bridge. Those of us who like adventures took advantage of the fallen tree and crossed the "bridge" cautiously and courageously. I, a person with height fright, did not take the risk. An hour later, we got out of the woods. It was such an exciting workout! The hiking was not at all boring. You do not need to listen to an iPod or MP3 while hiking in the woods. The chirping of birds is a natural symphony of joy.

Boat rides are a must for camping near a lake. Kids especially enjoyed water tubing. The driver wanted to drive the boat fast in a circle to spin out of kids in the tube. The kids tried their best to hang on to the tube. Of course, the boat driver was always the winner. However, spinning out of the tube, falling into the water, screaming like crazy, these kids enjoyed every minute of the excitement. They all came ashore beaming with smiles.

As sun started to set, we all felt tired. To end the day, we wanted to catch some fish for a delicious fish soup. Fishing is not easy as it often looks. We went fishing by the lake shore. The curtain of evening started to fall but none of us had any luck. Empty handed, we had to return to the camp site and had dinner without a fish soup. What a disappointment!

The two nights camping trip was short and sweet. Sunday was time for us to leave. As I started to dismantle the tent, clean the site and pack everything, I felt somewhat attached to the site. I temporarily owned the site. It was my home for two nights. My neighbors were my friends. We lived in a community, having activities together, eating together, and having fun together. The experience was very positive. Camping is an effective way to peel kids away from TV and game consoles. Camping provides an excellent opportunity for family and friends to socialize. Camping takes you away from work stress by brining you close to nature. I look forward to another trip next year. I proudly announce that I am now a member of nature loving camping club!

9 HAPPY HALLOWEEN!

Originated in the 5th century BC, in Celtic Ireland, the custom of Halloween was brought to America in the 1840's by Irish immigrants. On October 31, as some story goes, the disembodied spirits of all those who had died throughout the preceding year would come back, scavenging for living bodies to possess for the next year. The dead wanted to find their afterlife. All laws of space and time, as the Celts believed, would be suspended during this time, allowing the spirit world to intermingle with the living.

Naturally, not wanting to be possessed, villagers would extinguish the fires in their homes to make the living environment harsh for the spirits. They would then dress up in ghoulish costumes and parade around the neighborhood as noisily and destructively as possible in order to frighten away spirits looking for bodies to possess.

Today, the tradition has evolved into one of the spookiest holidays in America. It has been ritualized as a fun-driven celebration, characterized by colorful costumes, spooky decorations, and trick-or-treat activities.

House decoration is always part of the celebration. Charged with holiday energy and pumped by "ghost spirit", many families work hard on their Halloween decoration projects. It is such a visual feast to see the creativity and variety in the decorations in my neighborhood or others. I have seen families carving a jack-o-lantern and lighting it on the porch, front steps, or in a window. I always appreciate the traditional decorating objects such as cornstalks, haystacks, straw-filled scare crows, and last but not least, pumpkins. Now, it is common to see more modern objects such as air-filled nylon fairy-tale castles, and scary figures such as monsters, ghosts and witches.

Carving pumpkins has always been great fun to me. Although each family may choose a different decoration theme, a favorite component of decoration is to carve pumpkins into scary heads and place them in front of or around the front door. Some families may purchase plastic pumpkins with lights inside; others prefer to buy pumpkins from grocery stores or from a farm. Finding the best pumpkins for carving is never a problem for me. Being artistically challenged, however, I often scratch my head in trying to make my master piece the spookiest of all in my neighborhood. Of course, I never succeeded in my attempt. I am just not born with the natural talent to exaggerate an artistic expression to the extent I want. The Internet has come to the rescue of those with artistic deficiency. You can surf the Internet and find an image you like and lay it over a pumpkin. You can then complete your project like a master sculptor with tools that can be easily bought in grocery stores. Over the years, by getting inspirations from others, my design has improved tremendously. However, each year I discover unique ways of carving pumpkins from other families. If there are nine different ways to skin a cat, there are a hundred ways to carve a pumpkin into a vampire head.

On the night of trick or treat, I always enjoy watching costumes, especially those worn by children. You can wear whatever costume you like. I have seen girls dressed up as fairy-tale characters such as Cinderella, and boys dressed up as Captain Cook. Some wear the jerseys of their favorite sports team. Some like to be a movie character like Superman, Spiderman or Ninja. There is really no limit to your imagination. Whatever variety of costumes you see on a Halloween day, there is no lack of witches, vampires, skeletons and other scary figures. After all, Halloween is a spooky tradition!

The best part of Halloween is going on a trick or treat trip, at least for kids. Kids are kids. They love candies. Nowadays they do not get a chance to eat as many candies as they wish. Parents are concerned about their kids' health, especially the damage candies can do to their children's teeth. Halloween, however, makes an exception! It is the only time in the whole year when kids can get a boatload of candies. The magic words for getting your candies are "trick or treat". Literally, it means if you do not give me a treat (candy), I'll give you a trick (a mean one). House owners naturally would prefer to hand out treats to children to avoid mean tricks.

Each time I accompany my daughter Madison on her trick or treat trip, I cannot help but flash back to my childhood. "Trick or treat" in a way is very similar to the Chinese way of getting candies during the Chinese New Year. Instead of "threatening" the host with a trick, we would please the host with a "Happy New Year" greeting. We would put on the best behavior to get candies from those families we visit. In those years, if we could fill one pocket with candies, it would be a pleasant surprise.

Americans are generous to kids. American kids are being "greedy" on Halloween. After all, that's the only chance of the entire year to collect candies. Naturally, kids on a trick or treat trip will carry a sizable container that can hold several pounds of candies. Some older children even carry with them big bags. Each community usually has an arranged date for the trick or treat event. House owners are advised to turn on their door lights if they invite children to visit their houses. A family member usually sits at the door with candies by the chair. Kids' strategy to get most candies is more or less the same. They will start with one end of the community, going from door to door, to collect candies. If you live in a small community, you can drive your kids to a larger community so there are more houses to visit. I have never seen children happier than when they see candies dropped in their containers. A trick or trick trip usually lasts 2 hours. Most young kids, however, get exhausted in the end because of a two hour marathon walking from house to house.

To some, topping all the fun and excitement of Halloween may be visiting a haunted house. I have never entered a haunted house myself, even though there is one near my community each Halloween season. Visitors with heart problems or too young are advised not to embark on the adventure. I am perfectly healthy, but I have never been courageous enough to be tortured by all the creative means of scaring people to death. I would rather image how scary it would be inside the creepy house. I would "gloat" over those people who scream their way out of the haunted house. Such is life that "torture" can be extreme fun experience. Otherwise, why would so many kids or adults visit a haunted house?

10 A SPECIAL TRAFFIC COP

It was fall time. On the way to work, I was entranced by the signature autumn beauty in Northeastern Ohio: a world of colors created by the leaves that are to fall to the ground as winter sets in. Northeastern Ohio boasts a variety of trees whose leaves are so colorful in fall that it makes you marvel at the beauty God bestows on earth. The colors are too rich and picturesque for the human naked eye to miss. Unless you are color-blind, you will enjoy the annual seasonal visual feast.

I took out my cell phone and captured the natural beauty as I was driving along in good mood. Soon, to my dismay, I noticed cars slowing down to a halt in front of me. "Damn it!" I ran into another traffic jam. Traffic jams are nothing out of the ordinary in America. Typically, you would see traffic jams at highway merging sections or at highway ramps. Bad weather, car accidents, and road construction are also common causes of slow moving traffic. When there is a traffic accident, you just have bad luck. If you can take a detour to skip the jam, you would be lucky.

However, this time, the jam occurred on a road with a speed limit of 45 miles. There were no police cars flashing lights, no fire trucks, and no road construction signs. The weather was gorgeous! As I moved slowly and patiently forward, I caught sight of a turkey in the middle of the road, spreading its tail like a peacock, calmly cutting his way through the cars moving in both directions, as if he were directing the traffic. What an elegant turkey! Or rather what a beautiful traffic cop! The turkey was enjoying every minute of his show time. He was not scared at all. He was standing right in the middle of the road, watching the traffic from both directions passing by. Nobody sounded the horn to scare the turkey away. Every driver seemed to be happy to get such a close look at a wild turkey "directing" traffic. If he moved to the left side, the drivers on the right side would move slowly past the turkey or vice versa. When it was my turn, I pulled down the car window and snapped a few pictures of the turkey peeking at me. With his head up, neck stretched, he looked a bit arrogant. "Drive carefully!" The turkey stared at me, as if cautioning me about the traffic slowdown. Amazingly, drivers on the road obeyed the traffic cop's order respectfully. I did not know how long the traffic cop stood on duty, but it was one of the most memorable and hilarious experiences I had in my life. It was incredible to see how humans reacted to the turkey traffic cop, who probably received more civil obedience than a human traffic cop.

Having lived in Northeastern Ohio for so many years, I know Americans love animals. I heard many stories about people getting emotionally attached to pets such as dogs and cats, which are treated with human care and respect. Seeing so many drivers moving cautiously by a turkey gave me a unique perspective on Americans' love and respect for animals. The same can be said of Canadian geese. There are plenty of Canadian geese in Northeastern Ohio area. It is not uncommon to see Canadian geese crossing a road in a gaggle, holding their heads high, making goose steps, as if performing a military parade. American drivers respect geese rights to cross the road. They usually can tolerate the time it takes for geese to cross the road. Ironically, sometimes a driver behind me may blow his/her horn impatiently when I move a bit slowly. I really admire animals for the preferential treatment they enjoy from Americans!

When I shared my observations about Americans' love for animals with my friend Nancy, a retired school teacher, she did not seem to be satisfied with Americans' behavior towards animals. "They have not done enough!" she remarked. "Look at the dead animals on the road every day! It's terrible!"

There is some truth to Nancy's remark. For instance, raccoons are often run over by cars on the road. Being nocturnal, raccoons sleep for most of the day and are active during the night. Once I was driving home on a two lane road around midnight. As soon as I saw a raccoon 100 feet away creeping out from the shrubs along the side of the road, I stepped on the brake instantly. The raccoon, however, did not run away. Instead, it crouched low to the ground, staring at my car. As I moved slowly forward, the cute animal probably sensed the imminent danger, and crept across the street. I believe because raccoons are not easily noticeable at night, they become frequent victims on the road. In contrast to deer, raccoons are too weak to cause any damage to cars. Otherwise, there would be signs like "Raccoons X-ing" similar to "Deer X-ing" along the road. Poor raccoons, not all animals are born equal.

11 ADOPTING JOJO

Raising pets has never been my hobby. In spite of repeated pleading from my two daughters Sally and Madison, I have not changed my objection to having a cat at our house. However, Madison never gave up her efforts to convince me of adopting a cat. She did all the research online to show she was both mentally and physically prepared to adopt a cat. She promised me that she would be responsible for taking good care of the cat if we adopted one. However, none of her reasoning was strong enough to sway me to her side. Moreover, my wife was on my side, too. We did not want the extra burden to feed a cat. From cleaning the litter box to feeding, it would be lots of time commitment and responsibility like raising a baby.

Madison had been talking about adopting a cat for a year. She would bring up the topic whenever she could, whether it was on the way to her tennis practice or during our casual conversations at home. She literally bombarded me and her Mom with the same question "When can I get a cat?" multiple times a day. She was smart in asking when she could get a cat not whether she could get a cat. She made us feel it was just a matter of time rather than a matter of approval or permission. I had to admit that she had the way with words. She probably could be an excellent debater when she grows up.

I knew Madison loved pets. She would share with me her excitement of holding a cat or walking a dog at her friend's house. She was very knowledgeable about cats. Sometimes, I was on the edge of saying "Yes", but my wife pulled me back from supporting the decision. Other times, my wife was on the verge of approving the adoption, but I voted "No". So the adoption topic continued in our family on and off for quite a while without a consensus. It appeared that Madison's plan to adopt a cat would go nowhere.

One day, however, Madison pleaded with me and touched me so much that I changed my mind. Just two days before my birthday, Madison sat by me and said, "Dad, I feel lonely when I come back from school. I need a companion to talk to and play with. Can you please let me adopt a cat? Please! Please!!" All of a sudden, I felt emotionally connected with Madison. "How can I deprive Madison of the right not to feel lonely?" I thought to myself, with tears appearing in my eyes. Her pleading was so simple and powerful that I could not sit any longer. The impulse to adopt a cat was growing stronger and stronger in me. Something was burning inside me--I must fulfill Madison's wish without further delay!

So, without consultation with my wife, I took Madison and Sally, who was always supportive of adopting a cat, out on a search journey for a cat. I was concerned that my wife might burst into rage at me making decision without her. She had been adamant that she did not want a cat at our house. The burning desire to bring a cat home outweighed my concern. I would explain to her the decision after the fact.

We first visited the Cleveland Animal Shelter Center. The moment we entered into the room filled with cats in cages, Madison got thrilled. We knew what we were looking for—an indoor black kitten. We had had an adult black cat Booboo for a couple of years. The cat was brought home by Sally. Sadly, Booboo, an outdoor cat, was run down by a car while running across a road. Interestingly, black color had become our color of choice for cats. It might be because all of us were sentimentally attached to Booboo. His black color became our preference. But we would like to have an indoor cat this time. We could not afford to see another outdoor cat die tragically. Booboo was brought home as an adult cat. We missed all the fun and love of bonding with a kitten. So we decided to adopt a black baby cat or kitten so that we could train the kitten and develop a good relationship with the kitten. I often marvel at cats and dogs. They are so human. They are your companions. They are your daughters and sons. If you love them, they love you, too.

As we were looking around, one black kitten, named Slush, caught Madison's eyes quickly. He looked lonely and sad. He just had some eye surgery. He was only 4 months old and was found abandoned on a street. Madison held Slush to her chest. Amazingly, Madison and Slush clicked instantly. Slush gently stretched his arms to hug Madison's neck, his eyes staring at Madison, as if begging Madison to take him home. The touch, the love and the care Madison showed to Slush deeply moved me, sending a sense of guilt down my spine. How could I put out Madison's burning desire to adopt a cat? As her father, I regretted that I had not fulfilled Madison's wish sooner.

As Madison was still bonding with Slush, I noticed rashes on her face and around her neck. Madison was allergic to Slush's hair. The lady working at the facility there recommended that Madison not adopt Slush out of concern for her health. I tried to convince Madison not to adopt Slush. But the short period of bonding between Madison and Slush seemed already to have grown too strong to break. Madison really fell in love with Slush at first sight. She was already attached to Slush. Slush's hug was special. She wanted to take him home badly. In the end, I persuaded Madison to visit another animal shelter to see if we could find another kitten to her liking.

With great reluctance, Madison put Slush back into the cage and said good-bye to Slush, tears in her eyes. After 20 minutes' drive, we found another animal shelter in Parmer, a neighboring city of Cleveland. Again, I was amazed to see so many kittens in a long, narrow room filled with cages. Some kittens were adorable, others were cute, and still others were friendly. Their eyes seemed to be conveying one consistent message: take me home. I saw a sign saying "Take us home, please!" next to the cage with twins. For some reason, what I had seen at the Cleveland shelter and the Palmer shelter touched my heart. I felt much closer to cats. I started to understand why people love pets. Pets are like humans. They have feelings. They love you and want to be loved. They need a home of their own. As I was going through the emotional change, Madison and Sally settled on a cute black kitten. He was four months old and looked like Slush, too. We were all happy about the choice. Since this was Madison's cat, she renamed the cat as "Jojo". After completing all the paper work, we set out on the way home, filled with joy over the addition of a new family member to our home. It was truly a productive day.

To our pleasant surprise, my wife burst into joy instead of rage the moment she saw Jojo walking on the floor. She had been stubbornly opposed to adopting a cat. At least she had sounded so to us. Evidently, deep in her heart, she loved cats, too. Having raised two daughters, she just wanted to take a break. She knew raising a cat is like raising a baby—lots of time commitment and responsibilities.

Not experienced in raising a kitten, we put Jojo's bed, food, water and toys in the family room so we could see him easily. To our surprise, Jojo would run behind our sofa, hiding from us. He was playing the game of seeking and hiding with us. We got him out, and he would go back in once we put him down the floor. After feeding Jojo with a good kitten meal, Madison put Jojo on his own bed, a round nest-like cushion, specially designed for cats. We ended the day with joy and fatigue.

The following day, I got up early as I usually would. Jojo was gone! Madison was woken up by the bad news. She and I started the search mission. From each room to the basement, from under the sofa to behind the doors, we searched every possible place in our house without luck. Madison looked worried. I was puzzled. "Where could Jojo have been hiding?" Tired of searching, I fell into the sofa for a break. To my pleasant surprise, I felt a soft scratch on my back. It was Jojo inside the sofa back! We turned the sofa over. There we saw Jojo's eyes, apparently scared. No matter how we tried to persuade him to come out, he would not. Several times, he did reach his paws out, but the passage into the back of the sofa was too narrow for me to pull Jojo out by force. Frustrated, I started to push the back cover top down, slightly increasing pressure as I moved my hands down. Magically, Jojo came out timidly, as if he understood my pushing was the ultimatum for him to come out. Researching the Internet, I found that kittens need time to get acclimated to new environments. They like to hide under or behind sofas for the first few days. It is normal behavior. Knowing where Jojo would hide, we were no longer worried. As expected, in three days, Jojo felt at home, starting to explore the new environment with curiosity and ease. He felt completely welcome. He would play with his toys joyfully. He would jump onto Madison's laps to take a nap. He would follow me upstairs and downstairs.

Jojo is special. He is not just Madison's companion. He is another family member of ours. He now has a place he can call home. I am now absolutely happy about our decision to adopt Jojo.

12 THE APOLLO INSURANCE COVERS

Neil Armstrong, the first person to walk on the moon, passed away on August 25, 2012. The entire country was saddened by the loss of a hero who led the Apollo 11 mission. Memory of the glorious Apollo journey to the moon in 1969 came back live to many Americans who had witnessed the historic event. Armstrong was a house-hold name. He was an American hero. He inspired generations of Americans, invoking their pride about the greatness and power of the United States of America. I admired him for his courage and heroic feat. I was sad to hear the loss of such a great legend.

Armstrong's death prompted me to learn more about the hero. I was too young to understand the significance of Armstrong's flight to the moon in 1969. China was not open to the outside world, either. Most Chinese then did not have the privilege of watching the moon walk on TV. I barely had any memory of Chinese talking about the event. China then was buried in the revolutionary fire of the Cultural Revolution. What was happening on the moon was less relevant to Chinese than what was happening on their homeland. Moreover, why would the Chinese government be interested in reporting the huge success of the imperialist America? I, who witnessed the Cultural Revolution, missed the opportunity to see the greatest human achievement in space exploration.

To replay history and feel the pulse of the Apollo era, I started to read about what had happened on July 20, 1969, the date when the whole world watched in awe the epoch-making moon walk by Armstrong. There was no lack of news report about the mission. Americans then were proud of Armstrong just as Chinese were proud of Yang Liwei, who was the first to orbit around the earth in China. Reading the history, watching the videos and listening to the audios, I felt pages of the Apollo history flashing through my mind vividly one by one. Wasn't it amazing that human space exploration could go as far as the moon? Even more incredible was that this happened in 1969!

While reading about Armstrong's life, I encountered a news report that Armstrong was not able to afford life insurance. I could not believe my eyes. The story was simply absurd to me. As I read on, sadly enough, it was a true story.

After all the danger, glory, and fame, Armstrong, working for NASA, was no different from ordinary federal employees. As such, he was subject to the same General Schedule (GS) pay scale as everyone else ranging from typists to CIA agents. Believe it or not, a federal salary wasn't enough for Apollo 11 astronauts to purchase life insurance. Chinese may find this incredible, but it was the American way. Back in the 1960's, astronaut captains made about $17,000 a year, and a life insurance policy for Neil Armstrong would have amounted to $50,000 a year, or more than $300,000 in 2012 dollars. Astronauts are engaged in inherently risky business. As such, they have to pay much higher premiums. Fortunately, NASA worked out a simple, smart, and creative way to insure Apollo astronauts.

Approximately one month prior to the Apollo mission, Neil Armstrong and two other astronauts were locked into a room together and signed hundreds of autographs on envelopes emblazoned with various space-related images. The "covers" would, as the logic behind this suggested, become intensely valuable should the trio perish on the mission. We all believe that what is rare is precious. Envelopes autographed by the trio would no doubt be of special interest to collectors. Today, these covers are referred to as "Apollo Insurance Covers". To maximize the value of the covers, the crew put stamps on them, and sent them in a package to a friend, who dumped them all in the mail so that all the covers would be postmarked July 16, 1969 — the day of the mission's success — or its failure. Fortunately, the trip went off without a flaw. All three astronauts returned to earth safe and sound. They all enjoyed longevity and lived healthy lives. They all remained alive until Neil Armstrong's death on August 25, 2012. The average value of the covers in 2011 was estimated to be around $5,000 according to Collectors Weekly.

Stories like this often make me wonder about America. How come the richest country in the world would not pay an astronaut's life insurance policy? How come the most powerful country in the world would resort to the <u>Insurance</u> Covers? Why would the American government embarrass its national heroes to the outside world? The premium for an astronaut's life insurance policy was a tiny drop in a huge NASA's financial bucket. If NASA had spent so much training an astronaut, why was it not willing to take care of the life insurance matter for its astronauts? This is the country that sent the first person to walk on the moon. This is the country that invented the space shuttle. This is the country that put Hubble Space Telescope in orbit. This is the country that engineered the Curiosity's travel to Mars. The technological marvels in America have won respect and admiration from all over the world. To non-Americans, the Apollo Insurance Covers seem to take away some shininess from the halo of America. It may strike you as pathetic that an astronaut like Armstrong could not even afford his life insurance.

I was not alone to be perplexed by the fact that Armstrong was not able to afford his life insurance policy. My Chinese friends were surprised when I told them the story. Well, if you change the perspective and look at the story the American way, you will understand the cleverness behind the Apollo Insurance Covers.

The American government treats federal employees the same way. Working for the federal government, you have to pay out of your own pocket the premium for the life insurance policy for your family. It is not that the government is stingy or cannot afford the expense for astronauts. They have already spent millions of dollars training astronauts. It is that the policy of employee benefits is and should be applied fairly and consistently to all federal employees. Armstrong, together with his fellow astronauts, was no exception to the policy. Americans respect rules. Fairness is derived from "playing by the same rules". The Apollo Insurance Covers are just another reminder that the American way and the Chinese way are different ways. Watching American society through Chinese lens is not the same as watching it through American lens or vice versa.

13 THREE BLUE-EYED MONKS

On a mid-August day, 2003, I was driving my family from Ohio to Florida for a weeklong vacation. The weather was still scotching hot. The lingering heat would not go away. It was the first long driving trip we had taken since I came to America in 1990. A good portion of my driving was on the Interstate 95 (I-95) Highway, the main north-south land-based transportation corridor on the east coast. It is the busiest, most well-known, and arguably most important highway in the USA. Driving on highways for hours is not something you yearn for. It is monotonous and exhausting. As tired as I was, I concentrated on driving and was anxious to get to our destination, Daytona Beach, one of the beaches in Florida.

Passing West Virginia, North Carolina, South Carolina and then Georgina, we finally got in the Florida territory after 14 hours' drive. About 10 miles away from Daytona Beach on the Interstate 95, I suddenly felt the steering wheel vibrating like crazy. "What's the noise?" shouted my wife. She was freaking out. The two daughters got scared, too. I could hear a loud rumbling noise coming from the right front tire. "We must have got a flat tire!" I responded with calm, feeling certain about what happened. The steering wheel continued to vibrate badly as the car was rumbling along. "Damn it!" I blurted out angrily. "Why did it happen on the busy highway?" It was also the first time I had got a flat tire. A bit nervous, I eased my car cautiously over to the shoulder of the road so as not to cause irreparable damage to the car. The drivers behind and next to me were kind enough to slow down. So I could switch to the right lane. I carefully got out of the car, thinking that I would replace the flat tire with the spare tire. I had seen others replace tires on the road shoulder before. It looked simple, plus I had the right tools in the trunk. Generally considered a handy man by wife and friends, I was eager to try it out.

"Don't worry! It's just a flat tire. I'll replace it with our spare one", I comforted my wife and two daughters with professional confidence, as they got out of the car.

They were happy to be out, breathing fresh air, stretching their legs, even though it was sweltering hot. As I jacked up the car, I had trouble removing the flat tire. The nuts refused to come off. After a few more attempts, I was frustrated by my inability to get the job done. The confidence I had shown a moment ago was soon replaced with frustration. A sense of shame fell on me because I was not able to perform a typical DIY job. It's time to seek help.

Cars were zipping by in both directions. Looking around, I found an emergency road phone stand about 500 feet away on the road side. I ran to the phone, out of breath. I was going to call for the road service. Just as I was going to pick up the phone, I noticed a pick-up truck pulling slowly over to the telephone stand. A bald, bulky man jumped off the truck driver's seat, wrapped in a cape. Two more men were lying on the truck, relaxed. With heavy whiskers, the man looked intimidating, and the odd pattern on the cape intensified my angst about what would happen. Without a word, the man approached me with a disarming smile.

"Do you need a phone?" he asked politely, reaching out his right hand with a cell phone.

I had a cell phone with me, but I did not have the number to call for the road service. That's why I was going to use the emergency road phone. I guess the man thought I needed to make a phone call. He was offering me a cell phone to use. For whatever reason, I did not trust the man. Why should I trust a stranger? What if this was his scheme of ripping me off with excessive charge for using the phone? The thought of him and the other two fellows robbing us sent fear down my spine. I could hardly wait to get out of the situation. I reminded myself that provoking a stranger was the last thing to do. As he was stepping closer, I started to back away from him, waving my hand, signaling to him "I don't need your phone". I did not want to be rude, as that might rub him the wrong way. Much to my amusement, he thought I did not understand English.

Gesticulating in the air, the man tried to show that he could help me. I did not understand his gestures fully, but started to feel more threatened as he moved within my reach.

I hurried back to my car. But the man reversed his truck to my car.

"Can I help you replace the flat tire, sir?" the man offered his help kindly.

I was now in a hole, helpless. How could I refuse the offer? Moreover, he did not behave like a robber.

"Yes, please!" I answered with humbleness.

The three men started to work like a professional road service team. I was impressed by the man's muscular arms. The stubborn nuts did not seem to bother him at all. While I was watching them replacing the flat tire, I was at first ashamed of myself for not being strong enough to take the tire off. But I acted like Ah Q[1], thinking that they were people who would work with their hands but I would be best suited for working with my mind[2]. The man, with the help of the other two, finished the job in 15 minutes. I was so thankful that I wanted to pay them for the service, which was like bringing the much needed charcoal in snowy winter.

"How much would you like me to pay for the service?" I asked, showing great appreciation.

"Nothing!" the man rejected flatly.

"I'll feel bad unless I pay you!" I countered.

"Don't worry! We've done this many times. It's a pleasure helping people out."

I was curious about the capes all three men were wearing. "What do you do for a living?" I asked.

"We are monks. We are on the way to a concert to raise money for our temple."

"Holy Cow!" I murmured to myself. No wonder they were so happy to do good deeds.

"Well, you do accept donations, right?" I was still trying to find a way to pay them for their service or good deed.

"Yes," the man agreed, smiling.

I handed him a 50 dollar bill, saying "Thank you guys so much!"

The moment he took the bill, the man knelt down quickly and kissed my toe gently. I was speechless, totally puzzled by such an unexpected way of showing appreciation. To me, monks typically would "nian jing"(recite scriptures) and say "Er Mi Tuo Fo". The fifty dollars must have meant so much to him. Or monks with blue eyes have their own rituals.

Every time I share this story with my Chinese friends, they would say "you were rescued by a living Lei Feng". I cannot agree with them more. The world would be much nicer if there are more of people like these blue-eyed monks.

Note 1: "Ah Q" is a character in Lu Xun's "The Story about Ah Q". Ah Q is best known for taking a positive attitude to a personal defeat.

Note 2: From Confucius teaching

:

14 BUY ONE GET THREE FREE

When we lived at Allerton Apartments near Kent State University, Ohio, cats or dogs were not permitted. Fish and hamsters, however, were allowed. I had never raised a pet in China, and as a graduate student at Kent State, I had no desire to raise one. I was not ready to make the commitment and take on the responsibility. I was so focused on school work and research, as most Chinese students would be.

Things started to change as our daughter Sally grew older. A fourth grader, she started to show interest in pets. Her crave for a pet was growing fast and strong. She was no longer content with a few gold fish we had in a small fish tank. She wanted a pet she could play with. Each time she went to a friend's house, she would bug me for a pet. She knew cats and dogs were out of the question, so she pleaded with me for a hamster. Kids love companions. Pets help develop their care for animals. There are indeed many benefits of raising a pet at home. Hopefully, kids will develop a sense of responsibility for their pets just as we parents raise children. It is perhaps not an exaggeration that raising a dog is like raising a kid. It's tons of work! Hamsters, however, are not that bad. They live in a cage. They cannot run around in the room. So, I was not really opposed to the idea of bringing home a hamster. I would not consider it a crazy idea. Moreover, I have seen hamsters at friends' home. They are adorable and cute. It did not take long for me to warm up to the idea of getting a hamster. Sally was thrilled when I announced that we would get a hamster over the weekend. She shared the news with her friends. It looked like a big deal to her. She could not be happier.

To prepare for our new family member, I did research on how to raise a hamster. Hamsters were first discovered in Syria, but they are native to many parts of the world. The name they go by today is derived from the German word "hamstern," which means "hoard"—because that is exactly what they do with any extra food they might find. Hamsters are nocturnal by nature, so nightly digging, scratching and wheel-running by a hamster would be expected. Hamsters also have gained a reputation for biting, but they mostly tend to nip when awakened during the day—the time they are "biologically programmed" to sleep. Because of their nocturnal nature and tendency to nip, hamsters of any species are not appropriate pets for families with small children. Since Sally was a fourth grader, she was old enough to handle a hamster without being supervised by an adult. With the research done, I liked the idea of raising a hamster. It was a safe and happy choice for Sally, my wife and me.

On the morning of that Saturday, my wife took Sally to a nearby pet store. It was only 15 minutes' drive away from our apartment. Without much trouble, they brought home a cute hamster. A couple of days earlier, we had already prepared a home for the new family member. It was a small pink cage, with a running wheel inside, and a thick layer of aspen shavings at the bottom, which produce good smell and can be easily replaced when hamster urine or poop make them stink. A drinking tube was attached to a bottle of water so that the hamster could drink at will. The hamster was brought home in a paper bag. As soon as she was released into the cage, she got excited or perhaps scared or curious about the new home. The hamster got on the running wheel and started running while its eyes were inspecting the surroundings. "I like the new home! Thanks!" The hamster continued to run as if she appreciated our hard work. We spent at least an hour playing with the hamster. After all, we never played with such a cute fragile animal before. It was amazing how quickly human beings get connected with an animal. It appeared that the little thing clicked right away with us and was a perfect fit for our family. We named her Lulu.

About 10 days later, we got up only to find that the cage was empty. "Where is Lulu?" my wife screamed to me. "She escaped from the cage!"

"How could that be?" I shook my head, looking perplexed. I could not believe what had happened, but the cage was empty.

I was sure that the apartment door had been closed and locked because I was the last person to go to bed and I had a habit of locking the door before going to bed. I had never forgotten to do so.

"She has to be somewhere inside our apartment!" I comforted Sally and my wife. "There is no way she could get out of the room," I sounded absolutely confident.

We started searching behind the doors, and under the beds, but with no luck. It was so odd that a small hamster could escape from our room! Where could she be? Just as I was wondering about what possible places Lulu could be hiding, I heard some scratching noise from the bottom drawer of the kitchen oven. I suspected that Lulu was there. I carefully pulled the drawer open for fear of hurting Lulu. To the biggest surprise of my life, I saw three more cuties hustling around with Lulu. She just brought 3 more baby hamsters to the family! We were indeed excited, but we were totally unprepared for the added new members. "It's like buying one and getting three free," I joked with my wife, but I knew raising four hamsters would be more than we could handle.

My wife and I carefully placed Lulu together with her babies into the cage. I could tell it was a happy family. However, since then, the hamster family would not want to stay in the cage in evenings. Each day we woke up, we would find them in the same oven drawer. We would again put them back in the cage, but the next day they would end up in the drawer again. It was clear that when my wife, Sally and I went to bed, sometime during the night, they would escape from the cage and find their way into the drawer. The repetitive routine turned out to be too much for us. The simple solution to the dilemma was to give them away before we got sentimentally attached to the babies.

A day later, we put them in a big paper bag with a note attached to the handle, saying "Free hamsters for adoption!" We left the bag early in the morning at a noticeable spot on the parking lot before the pet store where we bought Lulu. Customers who were to buy hamsters from the store could easily catch sight of the bag. A couple of hours later, we came back to check on them. As we planned, they were gone!

15 DEER POPULATION CONTROL

I live in a suburban city called Hudson. Like other Northeastern Ohio suburban cities, the landscape of Hudson is picturesque. The city's area is about 5 miles in diameter. Woods are here and there within the boundary of the city. Wet land in the city is preserved for wildlife. Living here, you get a sense of being close to nature. It is one of the best and most beautiful residential areas in Ohio.

The wooded land is also a perfect place for deer. It seems that people and deer have cohabitated the area in harmony year after year. I have seen a few deer wondering on my neighbor's lawn or in our community many times. They look friendly, not at all scared unless humans approach them. Nobody in the community would react in any unfriendly way to scare the deer, even though they know these deer probably are the culprits for "trimming their plants". Last year, my wife planted a few green beans in the back yard. When the plants grew two feet tall, some deer visited our garden. All leaves of the green bean plants were gone! What would we Chinese do, seeing deer on our property? Deer meat would be a rare addition to dinner. The temptation to kill these deer could be too hard for some Chinese to resist. If that is too cruel, driving them away by yelling would be a reasonable reaction, especially when these deer eat the plants in your garden. I had no idea when the deer visited our garden. Even if I saw them eating the leaves, I could not shoot them, as that would be against the law. Moreover, I do not possess a gun anyway.

Deer are actually under protection by Ohio law. Is it because of the legal protection that Ohioans do not kill deer visiting their property or is it because they love deer just as love other animals? I believe the legal protection has allowed deer population to grow. Hunters, however, are permitted to kill deer at a designated hunting area if they have a valid hunting license. Americans are well known for their love for animals. The love usually goes to pets such as cats, dogs, hamsters, and birds, and so on. Deer are not considered pets. Hunters derive pride and excitement from shooting deer. In some hunters' house, you can see deer horns or head specimen hanging on the wall, a show of their hunting accomplishment. If there were no law preventing irresponsible killing of deer, the deer would have become an endangered species.

Because of the law protecting deer, deer population continues to grow each year, posing a headache to the residents. As deer population grows, they tend to cause more traffic accidents on the road. Deer like to cross the road on a sudden impulse. You never know when they will pop out from the road side, running across the road. If they walk across the road like a goose, they can safely cross the road. Americans treat animals well on the road. They yield to animals crossing roads. However, deer are deer. They would not listen to human advice on how to cross roads. They like to dash across the road. Once I hit a young deer crossing the road when it was rushing across the road without me noticing it. It was a young deer. All of a sudden I heard a heavy thumping noise originating from the bumper. Luckily, the deer made it across the road. It did not wreck severe damage to my car, either. From the noise, I guess the deer must have been injured, if not severely. Another time I was not lucky. The impact of hitting a deer was absorbed by the car hood, causing it to crumple up. In spite of signs posted along the roads where deer crossing is more often, each year I would see several deer lying dead on the road in the Hudson area and its neighboring cities. Across the country, the number of car accidents involving wildlife is estimated to be ranging from one million to two million per year. This estimate is based on insurance industry data. Human fatalities from wildlife related car accidents approach 200 each year. Most of wildlife accidents involve deer. For instance, in Pennsylvania alone, drivers struck approximately 97,000 deer in the last half of 2005 and first half of 2006, according to estimates by State Farm, the insurance company.[1]

So deer are both Americans' friends and trouble makers. Wildlife protection has strong support among American public. As friends, deer contribute to the optimal equilibrium of our living environment. As trouble makers, deer cause car accidents, which may result in human fatalities. Americans are in a dilemma—to kill or not to kill? Killing too many would break the equilibrium. Not killing deer would endanger human beings. Interestingly, some cities have figured out the optimal number of deer to allow within their boundaries. If the deer population growth exceeds the threshold, "licensed killing" is employed to control the growth. For instance, in the city of Hudson, Ohio where I live, when the deer population overgrows each year, the city would issue hunting licenses to the city residents for killing a planned quota of 500 deer. I do not know how they figured out the quota for hunters. You can infer from the quota that if these 500 are not killed, the deer population in Hudson will grow faster next year. If the growth is not contained, it will be a problem. So, it makes sense to kill some. Cruel, isn't it? Well, such is human hypocrisy that killing deer can be legal or illegal depending on when deer are killed and by whom. The harmony or peace with us humans is maintained at the sacrifice of the loved ones of the surviving deer.

Note 1: refer to the report by Jim Robins in the New York Times, December 22, 2007

16 FROM MELTING POT TO SALAD BOWL

The American writer Ralph Waldo Emerson used the "melting pot" image to describe "the fusing process" that "transforms the English, the German, the Irish emigrant into an American . . . The individuality of the immigrant, almost even his traits of race and religion, fuse down in the democratic alembic like chips of brass thrown into the melting pot." The melting pot metaphor has been well-known to us Chinese. Underneath the metaphor is an assumption that when you go to America, you are expected to assimilate yourself into the American culture.

Like other Chinese students, I came to America to pursue my American dream. The dream was pretty vague to me prior to my departure from China. Simply put, I yearned for a better life. In general, American dream refers to the ideals of freedom, equality, and opportunity traditionally held to be available to every American. In many cases, American dream is defined as a life of personal happiness and material comfort as traditionally sought by individuals in the United States. To many of us Chinese, American dream is quantitatively defined as having a job, a car and a house. To most of us, a master or doctoral degree is a stepping stone to the realization of American dream. With a degree, you are qualified for finding a job. With a decent salary from your job, you can buy a car. You can buy a house by borrowing money from a bank, especially if you have a reasonably good credit score. It does not appear unrealistic to have a job, own a car and live in a cozy house. Many of us Chinese students followed the same path and have successfully completed their journey of American dream. From having a valid working visa such as H1-B to a permanent resident card, the so-called "green card", and later to becoming naturalized as an American citizen, it is just a matter of time before you settle down in the country. Once you realize your American dream, you will have a solid financial footing to survive in America. The truth is that you have to earn your American dream. There is no free bread in America.

However, realizing your American dream is only a major milestone in life. It by no means shows that you have assimilated yourself into American society. The process of assimilation is a long and agonizing experience. You may try years after years to melt yourself into the American cultural pot only to find that something in you refuses to be melted. That's the cultural identity you have inherited from your Chinese ancestors. The Chinese blood still runs in your vein. You may dye your hair blond, but your skin will give you away. In other words, you jump into the melting pot a Chinese, you come out of the melting pot, still a Chinese, even though by nationality you have become an American citizen. The key to success is to embed yourself in the society you are living in, and to be a productive citizen without losing your identity and values.

As hard as it is to be assimilated into American society, we have all tried one way or another to be assimilated.

English is not our mother tongue. The language barrier is the primary challenge to assimilation. You have to be able to communicate well in English if you want to be part of American society. I could recall many moments when I wished I had been born here in America. Even if I had received formal English education in college, there were cultural subtleties that you could only understand if you were born and grew up here. It is usually an unattainable goal to achieve the fluency of a native speaker, especially for those of us adults who came to America past the optimal time for language acquisition. Mastery of slang or colloquial expressions is even tougher. In spite of all the challenges, with a few years of American education, plus working in America after graduation, Chinese can acquire English competency that is adequate for survival. Some may find it hard to get rid of Chinese accents, but accents do not bother Americans as much as we fear.

Americans like sports. Football, baseball and basketball are the three main sports known to the world. In the mid 90's, baseball was pretty hot in Northeastern Ohio because the Cleveland Indians were a winning team. I happened to be working at a bank in the downtown Cleveland area. I had never watched a baseball game in China, let alone played one. I had no interest in what was going on with the Indians' games. Each day I went to work, I felt the pressure from my colleagues, who would chat about the game played the night before. While my colleagues were talking zealously about the game, I was buried in my project work. Why would they waste time talking about sports? It's work time. I thought to myself. Sports are a big part of American life. Talking about sports is common at work place. Your peers, your boss, and your boss' boss, up to the executive leaders are engaged to different degrees in sports related conversations, especially at meetings. It's a good way to socialize with people. If you stay out of the main flow at work place, you will be left out. When in America, we should do as Americans do. So I started to watch baseball games at night. I convinced myself of the need to be knowledgeable about sports. I learned about the basics of baseball. I was happy to be able to join the baseball talk at work place.

One day, I went to work in an Indians' t-shirt to show my support for the Indians. Wearing an Indian's t-shirt had a dramatic effect. The moment I stepped into my cube, someone shouted with excitement: "Look, Jason is an Indians' fan now!" When I commented on how the Indians did the night before, my colleagues were thrilled. "Welcome to baseball, Jason!" I was accepted into their circle with warm welcome. However, my interest in baseball was not sustainable. It waned quickly as Indians' performance declined. Other than acquiring some knowledge about baseball, I never truly developed any appetite for baseball games. Baseball is too slow and boring to me!

I tried to develop interest in American football, too. Each year, during the Super Bowl event, football will dominate sports conversations. However, I could not keep my eyes on the Super Bowl game on TV for more than 10 minutes. I would watch the game a little bit simply to prepare myself for the next day conversation on the Super Bowl at work so that I would not look left out or ignorant about what my American colleagues care so much about. Talking about sports with colleagues is an effective way of building relationship with people at work.

All those years in America, my interest in ping pong has never waned. I have never given up my hobby, which I developed as a child. My friends and I play at the basement of my house regularly. In recent years, I developed a strong interest in badminton. I have been playing badminton for years at a fitness center with my Chinese friends.

We have tried to live and cook the American way. At times, we will eat sandwiches, plus salads. Other times, we will bake chicken legs. However, as Chinese, we like to do stir fries. Bread is convenient, but we prefer rice. Pizza is delicious, but we enjoy Chinese pancakes.

We have learned from Americans how to organize a potluck party, a picnic outing and Christmas gathering. We Chinese living in America have adopted American way of getting together for occasions. We celebrate

Halloweens by giving candies to kids meanwhile our own kids enjoy doing trick or treat at other houses in the neighborhood. We enjoy the day off on Thanksgiving, but we often substitute chicken for turkey. We decorate our Christmas trees like Americans, but we often fail to appreciate the significance of the holiday felt by Christians. Even though the festive atmosphere for mid-autumn festival celebration and Chinese New Year is nothing to be compared with what you see in China, we Chinese in America appreciate the occasions. We often invite American friends to join the celebration of Chinese specific holidays. We get the best from both cultures.

We have tried hard to talk like an American, eat like an American, live like an American and work like American. Yet, no matter how hard we have tried to assimilate ourselves into American society, we come out of the melting pot more Chinese than American. Our assimilation efforts have failed miserably.

With America becoming increasingly diversified, Emerson's melting pot metaphor has given way to the salad bowl metaphor. Researchers found that America is more like a big salad bowl filled with distinctive ingredients from different countries with different cultural heritages. It is this diversity that gives America unmatched strength in the world. You do not have to lose your cultural heritage to become an American. Each ingredient makes the salad taste good. America is like salad dressing blending all the ingredients together. The American society is becoming increasingly inclusive. Living in America, you feel like a global citizen, exposed to a variety of world cultures. The need to assimilate has been on the decrease. You do not have to lose your own identity and values to be successful in America. No matter what cultural background you carry with you to America, as long as you earn your American dream and abide by the law, you can contribute to American society.

17 GOOD FENCES MAKE GOOD NEIGHBORS

Americans respect personal space between each other. When an elevator booth is filled to its capacity, they would prefer to wait for the next ride. Staying too close to each other invades private space. Having lived in America for more than 25 years, I have never seen people here push their way into the elevator. When engaged in a conversation with an American, you are advised not to stay too close to the person you talk to. There is what I call an invisible fence between you and the person. The exact social distance between people varies from person to person and from situation to situation.

Hall (1966)[1] identified four zones that are common for Americans. They are the public zone, the social zone, the personal zone, and the intimate zone. The public zone, generally over 12 feet, is observed when we are walking around town, because we try to keep at least 12 feet between us and other people. For example, we will leave that space between us and the people walking in front. We will start to notice other people who get within this radius. The closer they get, the more we become aware and ready ourselves for appropriate action. Within the social zone, which is between 4 and 12 feet, we start to feel a connection with other people. When they are closer, then we can engage them in a conversation without having to shout, but still keep them at a safe distance. This is a comfortable distance for people who are standing in a group but maybe not be talking directly with one another. People sitting in chairs or gathered in a room will tend to like this distance. In the personal zone, which is 1.5 to 4 feet, the conversation gets more direct, and this is a good distance for two people who are talking in earnest about something. When the social distance becomes less than 1.5 feet, the person you socialize with is within arms' reach or closer. This intimate zone allows you to see more details of the body language of your counterpart. As such, it is perfect for romance of any kind. All the theory of social distance tells us is that it is important to keep people at a respectful and proper distance depending on the situation. Sensitivity to space is essential in social interaction with people.

Just as people maintain an appropriate social distance between each other, houses in a neighborhood are also properly spaced apart. Each city has its own building code to regulate land and housing development. In the city where I reside, for instance, a minimum of 50 feet between two houses is common in modern neighborhoods. The distance provides a decent private space for each family. It is good separation to prevent fire on one house from spreading to other houses. Noise from a party in one family may not disturb the peace of its neighbors. Unlike social distance, the distance between houses is fixed when they are built.

The distance implies that each family has its private property space. The owner of the property can put up a sign, saying "No Trespass on the Property", if the owner chooses to do so because it is the owner's property. It is generally not a good idea to walk on your neighbor's lawn, as it is an invasion of your neighbor's private property unless you are invited to walk across the lawn. When you host a party, you are expected to manage the noise, making sure it won't get too loud for your neighbors to bear. It is not uncommon for an American to call the police and complaint about the noise disturbing neighbors. Your guests must not block the driveways of your neighbors. If you raise a dog, you may install an invisible fence on your property so that your dog will not trespass onto your neighbor's property. This reminds me of Robert Frost' famous poem *Mending Wall* published in 1914.

The narrator of the poem is vexed by his neighbor's insistence that there has to be a fence between them. Unfortunately, his neighbor could not get beyond his father's beliefs – originating in an old proverb – "Good fences make good neighbors". From the surface, the poem's refrain seems to suggest that keeping space between people is good for relationship building. What Robert Frost really meant is not that good fences make good neighbors, but that boundaries are what alienate us from each other. Fences between houses in modern days are not common. More Americans like the open space.

However, when it comes to dogs, it is wise to install an invisible fence around your house. My former next door neighbor Mr. Smith raised a dog named Maggie. She was a beagle. **Small, compact, and hardy, beagles are active companions for kids and adults alike.** My neighbor and I got along very well. We would stop and chat about things while mowing our lawns.

My wife and his wife would exchange ideas about gardening in summer. Maggie, however, would often cross the border into my property and pee on my grass. At first I thought dog's pee would be good fertilizer to the grass, so I did not mind Maggie donating her urine to my grass. But soon I discovered that there were spots of dead grass on my law. It was no brainer that Maggie's urine was the culprit. This is because dog's pee contains alkaline urine pH and nitrogen load. I felt my property was invaded and "attacked". I needed to "defend" my property. Thinking that Maggie was innocent, I was not sure what to do. Dogs are dogs. You cannot blame a dog for bad behavior. You go after the owner. So, I decided to bring up the issue to my neighbor Mr. Smith.

"Mr. Smith," I greeted him warmly as I would normally do while he was walking Maggie in our neighborhood. "Did you notice the patches of dead grass on my lawn?" I went straight to the topic. There was no need to beat about the bush on this matter.

"Yes, Jason," he answered with a sense of guilt. "I would fix them for you over the weekend."

"Thank you!" I appreciated his understanding and willingness to repair the damaged grass. "Maggie is adorable. I did not know her pee can kill grass."

He kept his promise and patched the spots with grass patches. It was, however, only a temporary solution. Unless Mr. Smith chained Maggie to a tree on his yard, Maggie would continue to invade my property and pee on the grass. After all, dogs love freedom and enjoy running around. A few weeks later, I noticed more patches of dead grass. So, I approached Mr. Smith again and expressed my concern over the problem.

"Don't worry, Jason. I thought about the situation. I will install a fence. Good fences make good neighbors," he assured me humorously and sincerely.

"Excuse me," I was not excited about the idea. "Did you say 'fence'? It's your call but I am not sure I like that idea." I did not like the physical barrier separating us. It would make my property look half enclosed.

Sensing that I did not really understand what he had meant by fence, Mr. Smith said, "It's not a wooden fence. It's an invisible fence, or an underground, electronic pet fence."

What a relief! "That's an awesome idea!" I could not wait to see it installed.

Two weeks later, an invisible fence was installed on his lawn. It worked magic. After a period of training, the fence kept Maggie contained to his property. With the invisible fence, Maggie was able to exercise freely without getting out of the boundary. No wonder in our neighborhood most of the families who raise a dog have installed an invisible fence. It works perfectly! Good fences indeed make good neighbors!

[1]Hall, E.T. (1966). The Hidden Dimension, New York: Doubleday

18 RECALLING A GOVERNOR

It is not uncommon to hear manufacturers recall their defective products already sold to consumers in America. However, when I first heard about it in the early 1990's, I was perplexed by the news. Never before had I heard any recall in China. When I grew up in China, you would be lucky if you could return a product with defect to the store you had bought the product from, let alone seeing a factory voluntarily recall its products.

Well, as I learned more about the American society, I found it makes perfect sense for a company to recall its defective products that can potentially cause injury to consumers. America is a country, notorious for law suits. For example, if a GM's car is involved in a car accident due to a defect in its car, victims in the accident can sue GM for damages. American juries are generally more sympathetic to the victims. Once GM is found guilty, GM may have to pay huge punitive compensation to the victims. It is therefore more economical for GM to recall a specific car model once it is found to have a defect that can lead to accidents. So, recalling a defective product is a protective measure for companies to mitigate exposure to potential risks.

While it is easy to understand a product recall, I find it hard to understand a governor recall. The year 2012 witnessed a governor recall event unfold with enormous curiosity. Scott Walker, the Governor of Wisconsin State, pushed through a bill the year before that stripped most public workers of nearly all their collective bargaining rights. Walker insisted on making the changes to balance the state budget and give local leaders fiscal flexibility, but the move sparked a massive protest at the state Capitol that went on around the clock for three weeks. This was American democracy in action. The confrontation did not force Walker to budge. Walker's backers, mostly

Republicans and Walker's opponents, mostly Democrats, were locked in a heated debate. Well, when a debate spreads statewide or even nationwide, no side can determine the winner without resorting to election. That's how American politics works.

So, the Democratic Party tried to exact revenge by forcing Walker into a recall. The party succeeded in collecting enough signatures from voters to force a recall election. Meanwhile, Republicans across the country rallied around Walker, pouring millions of dollars into his campaign fund. Both sides campaigned fiercely. Tons of money, which is a key to winning election in America, was spent on campaign ads. The grassroots in the state were mobilized. The entire nation was watching closely the event unfolding. The stake was high for both Democrats and Republicans. Both sides channeled tremendous energy and efforts into the recall election. To the thrill of the Republican Party, on June 5th, 2012, Walker easily dispatched challenger Tom Barrett, a Democrat, becoming the first U.S. governor to survive a recall. Walker not only made history by winning a tough recall election, the winning spurred his rise to political stardom. He became an emerging star in national GOP circles through the recall.

In delivering the Gettysburg Address during the American Civil War, Abraham Lincoln took the opportunity to ensure the survival of America's representative democracy by making the famous statement that the "government of the people, by the people, for the people, shall not perish from the earth." Governors are elected into office by the people. They can also be elected out of office by the people. This is how democracy works. Americans may be polarized in their views, but they tend to accept the outcome of an election on issues. Does this mean Walker's bill was right because more people supported him? Well, it's not a matter of right or wrong. The bill was loved by some but hated by others. Walker luckily won more votes than his opponent. On the surface, the election looked fair. However, we humans are easily influenced by what we see and what we hear. No experts can measure how much influence a campaign ad has on voters, but experts agree that campaign ads are effective in changing the minds of swing voters. Millions and millions of dollars were poured into the election. I wondered if the election had actually been determined by money instead of people. It takes lots of money to run a campaign! Election is a fair game but today ordinary people cannot afford to play the expensive money game. Candidates often withdraw their candidacy because they run out of campaign funds. The candidate that laughs best may be the person who laughs last and has the deepest pocket.

19 TIPPING

Tipping is expected in the United States for service, especially in sit-down restaurants where waiters and waitresses serve customers tableside. Tipping is customary at other places such as nail salons, barber shops, beauty shops, and taxis, to name a few. Some restaurants print suggested tipping amount on the receipt for you, for instance, 15%, 18% and 20%.

Not everybody understands America's gratuity culture. A friend of mine, who used to work at an upscale American restaurant, told me that even British travelers, who are more accustomed to a discretionary tip of around 10% if they have enjoyed a meal, often find themselves in an awkward situation by not adhering to America's gratuity culture. Chinese, who do not grow up in a gratuity culture, find it harder to adapt to the tipping practice.

Not long after I came to America, I had an opportunity to attend an academic conference on English Rhetoric at University of Pittsburgh. I was one of the Ph. D students on the group. We planned to dine out at lunch time. It was my first time to go to an American restaurant. So when we found our way to an American native Indians restaurant, I was excited and eager to try some Indian food. I ordered a soup with Indian herbs, because everybody else on the group ordered soups. I had not dined at an American restaurant before. I had no idea about what to order. When in doubt, do as Americans do. The only restriction for me is meat. Since the soup was a vegan choice, I figured it should be fine. Much to my chagrin, it tasted too strong and weird for me. It tasted like Chinese herbal medicine and upset my stomach. My appetite was gone after a couple of spoonful soup. However, the American friends I dined with looked very happy. They clearly enjoyed their delicious orders, most of which were also soups with Indian herbs. Being nice and professional, the waitress did a great job taking care of our orders, refilling water, taking away used plates, and so on. In the end, we each pitched in 6 dollars. The menu price for my soup was only $4.99, so my tipping amount was $1.01, approximately 20%. Six dollars is by no means expensive. But the one dollar tip bugged me days after the conference. At least for me, the dining experience was far from being pleasant. What was the tip for? Was it for a good experience or a bad one? Since it was a group dining setting, I did not want to spoil the happy mood of the others by refusing to pay the tip. Moreover, the tip was meant to reward the server or waitress, whom I should not hold accountable for ruining my appetite. The fault was with my bad choice. The experience left a bad taste in my mouth. I wished that the restaurant had been one without tipping requirement. If I had just paid for the fixed menu price of $4.99, I probably would have felt better.

Well, there are always two sides of the same coin. A couple of months later, I went to another restaurant with some American friends. We were all hungry and placed our orders quickly. Of the five people, I and another person were vegetarians. We ordered vegan choices. It took a while for the waiter to bring us glasses of water. Admittedly, the restaurant was relatively busy at that time. Some waiting time is acceptable under the circumstance. The waiter came to our table a few minutes after servicing water. He took our orders one by one as waiters or waitresses typically do. When it was my turn, I ordered a salad, which usually comes with bacon. I specifically requested no bacon for the salad. When the orders came to the table, my order was messed up. It contained bacon, which I was allergic to. What's worse, I did not know it until I had the first bite. My stomach reacted to this strongly. I was on the verge of throwing up. Thanks God. I managed to hold down the "chemical reaction" inside. I called the waiter to the table and asked why the salad still contained bacon. Even though my order was replaced, I had to wait for 10 more minutes. It was an awful dining experience. The waiter for some reason did not listen to me carefully when I placed my order or he forgot that I told him not to add bacon. Since we went Dutch this time, each paying our own bill, I did not leave him with any tip. I wanted to show him that I was not satisfied with his service. At the moment I kind of liked the tipping practice. If I had paid the fixed amount, I would not have had the freedom to add or reduce the amount of gratuity. It was totally my decision. The gratuity can be proportional to the service quality provided by a waiter or waitress. My not paying him any tip sent a strong message to him that customers are kings. Kings don't reward servers for bad services.

Having lived in the culture of gratuity for so many years, I have learned to appreciate the tipping practice in America. It is simply a norm. I very much enjoy the privilege of deciding how much to pay depending on how satisfied I am with the service. Services do make a difference. It enhances your dining experience. You just have to think of the tip as an expense and factor tipping into your assessment of how expensive a restaurant is. Plus waiters or waitresses typically get a lower base pay. They make a living by earning tips through services. If I do not pay an adequate amount, I feel bad about exploiting their service.

20 GUANXI MAKES A DIFFERENCE

In China, you are blessed if you have some "guanxi" (connection) with people in power, especially with government officials who are in key positions. It would not be a surprise if most of us Chinese have used our "guanxi" at least once in our life to accomplish something. I used my "guanxi" to get the permission from the Jiangsu Provincial Bureau of Higher Education for me to come to America. I was considered, to my honor, a talented scholar that the authorities in concern would not want to let go to prevent the so-called "brain drainage". I used one "guaxi" to get another "guaxi" to speed up my passport application processing. In short, I took advantage of several of my "guaxi" to be able to come to America for further study.

People who use "guaxi" to get things accomplished are often described as having "tried the back door" (Zou Hou Men). In many cases, trying the front door leads nowhere. As I lived through the 70's and 80's as an adult, I was both a beneficiary and a victim of "trying the back door", which was prevalent all over the country. But I hated "guaxi" then, and still hate "guaxi" now. If the back door is not closed, people with guanxi would have an unfair advantage over those "guanxiless".

In the past dozen years, as more and more Americans went to China to explore business opportunities there, many of them learned "guanxi" the hard way. American business practice, which is mostly governed by law, does not always work in China. Not that China does not have law banning the back door, but that the guanxi culture is so deeply entrenched in China that it is impossible to succeed without building a good "guanxi" network In China.

I cannot imagine living a guanxi based life again. Without relatives and friends in our early years in America, many of us overseas Chinese did not have to turn to "guanxi" for help. We simply did not have any! We worked our way to become successful in America. I would often tout to my friends in China about the difference made by absence of guanxi in America.

However, nothing is absolute. In early June 2007, I applied for a US passport for a trip back to China. Due to the 9/11 terrorist attack in 2001, all travel outside the United States requires a valid passport. People who travel to Canada did not need passport before, but they all had to then. As a result, passport applications bombarded the passport processing agencies. The wait time on average was 45 days. This drove me mad because I had booked the flight for mid-July. I did not know it would take that long. As the departure date drew close, I called the agency every day, but the phone system was jammed by similar calls. The agency advised applicants to go online to check the status, but the status would remain "in processing". The impatient waiting and concern about missing the flight somehow reminded me of many situations I had been through in the guanxi world in China. "Would it be nice if I had some guanxi in America that could expedite my application processing?" I thought. "But this is America. Guanxi does not work," I said to myself.

When I shared my anxiety about the matter to my boss at work, he offered me a solution. His son booked a flight to Germany. He was in the same boat as I was. He called the congressman who represented his district and asked the congressman for help. Magically, his son's passport arrived the night before his departure the following morning. My boss's success comforted me and raised my hope for getting mine in time for the flight. I contacted my district's congresswoman's office. I was impressed by their willingness and kindness to help me out. The office clerk kept me updated every day, and my passport arrived one day before the departure. While I was appreciating their help, I asked myself "Is this the American way or the Chinese way? Is this an example of guanxi? "

As a person not interested in politics, I never knew who represented my district. But I was connected to her through election. I was one of the constituents that she would need to vote for her. It was her responsibility to help her constituents. I did not give her any present or money as an incentive for her to help me, but my vote was worth enough to get the service I needed. What if I had not contacted my congresswoman for assistance? In a way, "guanxi" also matters in America. Perhaps, we ordinary people in America can make our living without having to resort to "guanxi". When needed, "guanxi" does make a difference.

21 WHERE DID THE BEES COME FROM?

It was a Saturday morning. By the time I got up around 10 o'clock in the morning, it was already humid and hot outside. I had to water my lawn because the sweltering summer heat had been lingering in the area for a while. Grass was dried up and needed water badly. I did not have a sprinkler system for watering the lawn automatically. After a quick simple breakfast with cereal and milk, I started to water the lawn manually with a hand sprayer, attached to a long garden hose.

"What's up, Jason?" A pleasant greeting came from Steven, my newly settled next door neighbor.

"Not much. Another hot day," I complained, sweat already dripping off my forehead.

"What are up to?" I asked Steven, seeing him doing carpentry work on the driveway right in front of the garage.

"Well, I need to fix up the bookshelf in the study room," he looked content with the work in spite of the heat under the sun. He is a handy man. I was impressed by the finished basement project he completed by himself after moving into the house. He has been busy with home improvement projects since he moved here a few months ago.

"Great! Not everybody is a carpenter. I wish I could do it. My wife would be happy." I admired Steven for his ability to do it by himself. DIY (Do It by Yourself) is common in America, but carpentry work is not that easy to me, plus you need all the right tools.

"Well, I use my hands but you use your brain," Steven comforted me, trying not to make me feel inferior. I appreciated his emotional intelligence.

Steven was half naked with no clothes except a pair of shorts, due to the heat. The muscles on his arms looked like those on an athlete's arms with clear outlines. Standing next to him, I paled miserably as if comparing a chicken leg to a turkey leg. Anyhow, Steven was a modest guy and did not show off his masculinity even if I told him that he looked like a body builder. Sweat was streaming down his face like crazy. He was nevertheless happy with the project, showing no sign of retreating into the garage for a rest.

"Okay, I'll let you go and do your project. I will take a look when it's complete," I said, anxious to continue watering the lawn.

"You bet," Steven said. With that, the buzzing noise from the wheel saw started again.

"Ouch!" A few minutes later, I heard him scream with pain. I thought he had accidentally cut his finger.

"Are you Okay, Steven?" I rushed to his driveway. He was covering his left calf with his hands, agonizing over something.

"Damn! I got stung by a bee!" said Steven.

"Sorry to hear that. I got stung by a wasp last summer while moving the lawn. Not too bad," I tried to sympathize with him, showing my own emotional intelligence.

His calf did not swell that much, so he resumed his work.

As ill luck would have it, the next day, he got stung again in the afternoon. He started to suspect that there must have been beehives built by bees or wasps somewhere on his house. It could be on the roof, window or door corners. It got to be somewhere on the house. So his wife called a professional exterminator to spread some chemicals on the areas where beehives could be built. The treatment service cost Steven a couple of hundred dollars. But Steven felt much better, knowing that the danger of sting had been eliminated.

Apparently, the treatment worked. Steven was happy about the result since he was not stung the day after the treatment. The following day, I went to check on his project. "Ouch!" I screamed. I thought I stepped on a nail, hurting the toe of my right foot.

"What happened?" Steven asked.

Inspecting the hurting toe, I found that it was a sting by a bee or wasp. "I was stung by a bee or wasp!" I told him, looking upset.

"Are you sure? My house was treated a couple of days ago. I have not seen any bees since then," he said, not convinced that another bee or wasp was the culprit.

I started to look around and caught sight of a bee flying back to the cranberry tree at the corner of my house. The tree was about 30 feet away from Steven's work station outside the garage. I carefully got under the tree branches. Holy Cow! Up on a branch was a huge beehive, the size of a cylinder with 5 inches in diameter and 1.5 feet in height.

"Steven," I ran out, shouting. "Guess what I found?"

"What?" Steven walked towards me. He looked at the direction I pointed at.

"Aha! That's the real culprit," Steven was surprised to see the huge beehive.

The beehive was covered with bees moving around. I was afraid they could attack us any moment. I rushed home and brought a bottle of wasp killer. I aimed at the beehive and spread the foam over it as quickly as I could. One after another, the bees on the surface of the beehive started to fall off to the ground. In a few minutes, the bees were gone. The beehive was immersed in wasp killer foam. Any remaining bees inside the beehive probably would be dead for lack of oxygen or poisoned to death while trying to get through the foam. I wish I could have spared the lives of the bees. Given the danger of being stung, and the suffering Steven had sustained, I was anxious to get rid of the bees as soon as possible. To be on the safe side, I used a rake to pull the beehive off the tree and sealed it in a bag. I then tossed it into the trash can. If I had to get a professional service to handle it, I would have to pay for the service. I did not believe it was worth it. It was after all a DIY job I could handle. Not much muscle was needed.

After taking care of the bees, I felt a bit guilty of what had happened. What could I have done differently? I asked myself. Why did the bees choose my tree to build the huge hive? Was it because there were more flowers in our garden than in the neighbors' gardens? Should I have called pest control to get rid of it? How did Steven and his wife feel about the 200 dollars? Would they be upset with me? Regardless, it was beyond my control. I did not raise the bees. Poor Steven simply had bad luck.

I often reflect on this incident at work. We often make assumptions about things. The root cause of Steven's bee sting was the nearby beehive. The buzzing noise from the saw attracted the bees. Without thinking beyond his own property, Steven assumed the problem originated from his house. He spent $200 only to find the root cause was something else. If I had not got sting that day, would Steven have been stung more times? How would he have found the root cause? Unless you know the root cause of a problem, you cannot really fix the problem.

22 GENERAL TSO'S CHICKEN

One of the popular dishes on the menu of a Chinese restaurant in America is General Tso's Chicken. The first time I visited a Chinese restaurant with an American friend, I was embarrassed by his question on the origin of the dish.

"Jason, is General Tso's Chicken popular in China?" he asked.

"Bob, to be honest with you, I have never heard of the dish in China," I told my friend Bob. Feeling a bit embarrassed about not having the answer Bob was looking for, I chose to be honest.

"When I grew up there in the 60's and 70's, eating at restaurants was considered a luxury for working class families. Most people would cook at home," I tried to imply to Bob that I was not much exposed to Chinese cuisine and therefore did not know much about the history of Chinese dishes.

"But I know General Zuo was a famous Qing Dynasty general from Hunan. Maybe General Zuo or Tso as you Americans call him, liked the dish and somehow, the dish was named after the general," I offered my assumption to Bob.

"Well, why not ask the owner?" I thought to myself.

Just then, the waitress came over to add water to our glasses. She was a pretty young Chinese girl, with heavy Cantonese accent in her English.

"Excuse me," I asked. "Do you know the origin of General Tso's Chicken?"

"Sorry, I don't know," she answered, her face looking blushed a little bit. "Maybe the master chef knows," she added.

"Can you please ask the master chef if General Tso's Chicken was General Tso's favorite dish and named after him?" I politely requested.

"Okay," she promised and went back into the kitchen.

A couple of minutes later, she came back, walking to our table as if with an answer I was looking for.

"Sorry, the chef does not know anything about it?" The waitress's answer was quite disappointing.

It was an unreasonable expectation on my end that the chef would have the answer. After all, chefs at Chinese restaurants in America do not necessarily attend Chinese cuisine schools. They learn how to cook Chinese dishes on the job. Knowledge about the history or culture behind Chinese dishes is not part of their job qualifications.

For some reason, it bothered me not to have the right answer to my friend Bob. So, on the way out, I asked the owner.

"Excuse me, do you know why General Tso's Chicken is called that way," I asked, still hoping to get a satisfactory answer.

"No," he smiled. "It's a good dish. Americans like it a lot."

The dining experience was great, but the question had been lingering in my mind since then. It was somehow a mystery that a general in Qing Dynasty got associated with a chicken dish.

A few months later, Bob and I went to have lunch again.

"Do you still remember last time we tried to get an answer about the origin of General Tso's Chicken?" Bob asked, with his facial expression suggesting that he had something surprising about the topic to share with me.

"Yea, what about it?" I was curious what he had to share with me.

"You know, my friend just came back from Shanghai. He was so impressed by the tremendous economic growth in China. I would like to visit China in the future." Bob sounded very positive about the rapid changes in China.

I was of course happy to hear an American friend make positive comments about the achievements of China, my motherland.

"Yea, it's amazing how fast China has grown in recent years," I concurred with Bob. "But what does that have to do with General Tso's Chicken?"

"Good question. While in Shanghai, he ate at multiple restaurants but none of them offered General Tso's Chicken on the menu. At one of the upscale restaurants in Shanghai, when he ordered General Tso's Chicken, they were puzzled by his order. He was both embarrassed and surprised that they did not even know what he was talking about."

"That's interesting." I was a bit amused by his friend's experience. "I never heard about it in China when I grew up. It must be an American thing. The guy who invented the dish must have been a shrewd businessman.".

"Agree. That guy was smart," Bob echoed my opinion. "Name recognition helps."

"But how many Americans really know who General Tso is," I remarked. "Perhaps, it is the military rank 'general' that is appealing to customers."

"Yea, if General Tso liked it, it has to be good." Bob followed my reasoning.

I have been to many Chinese restaurants in America. I have not seen any famous names associated with Chinese dishes other than General Tso. Whatever the true story behind General Tso's dish does not matter much to Americans who enjoy eating the dish. It is perhaps better to keep the mystery. Zuo Zongtang is probably the most famous Chinese general in America. Americans may not know much about General Tso. The popular association of the chicken with General Tso will continue to stay as long as Chinese restaurants in America offer the dish on the menu.

23 CHINESE ALSO NEED A CALCULATOR

"How's your math test today?" I asked Yanyan, a high school student from mainland China, who temporarily stayed at my house. As her host family Dad, I would check how she was doing every day.

"Excellent," she answered with confidence. "But it's weird that the math teacher would not lend me a calculator today when I wanted to borrow one from him. I left mine at home. I needed one for the test. You know what? He said that 'Chinese students do not need a calculator'. I insisted that I needed one to do trigonometry problems. He then lent me one."

"Hmm," I was surprised to hear the story. "Is this fair for an American math teacher to treat a Chinese student like that?" I asked myself. "What's he thinking about Chinese students? Maybe, to his mind, they are math wizards?" The teacher's attitude was really disturbing to me. Whether his remark was serious or meant to be a joke, it was not appropriate or professional in the context.

I thought about lodging a complaint to the high school principal, but, on second thoughts, I felt he was perhaps innocent. Since Yanyan was the first Chinese student to attend the private high school, he must have read or heard about the stereotype about Chinese students' superiority in math. On the other hand, if I did not let him know the negative impact his stereotyping Chinese had on Yanyan, he could continue to use the same stereotype to victimize future Chinese students whether intentionally or unintentionally. So, I emailed a note to the teacher and pointed out frankly to him that it was not appropriate for an American teacher to let his or her judgment be influenced by stereotypes about Chinese. He appreciated my note and apologized for using the stereotype.

It is true Chinese students are known to be more rigorously trained in math, but not all Chinese students are mathematicians. It is absurd to think that a Chinese student will not need a calculator to do trigonometry problems. Each individual student should be assessed on his or her own merits whether the student is Chinese or not.

Unfortunately, such is human nature that we tend to form stereotypes about people based on our own experiences or anecdotes from others. We have a tendency to generalize things based on limited facts. When we see a white swan, we may jump to the conclusion that all swans are white. In spite of the flaws in our thinking logic, we are inclined to follow this thinking pattern. That's why stereotypes are common. It does not matter whether they are logical or scientifically proved or not. We humans like to establish stereotypes for others.

Once I attended a company training class on Diversity and Inclusion. The goal of the training was to help leaders recognize that the work environment was becoming increasingly diversified. Leaders should be mindful about the diversified work force. All employees, regardless of their cultural backgrounds, ethnic origins, religious beliefs, age, sexual orientation, etc. should be treated equally and respectfully. The company should cultivate an inclusive environment in which employees feel engaged and included. During the training, the instructor asked us to form a group of 6 and do an interesting exercise about stereotypes. Each of the attendees was asked to write down the stereotypes they know about Chinese, African Americans, Latinos, and Americans.

The two expressions that came to my mind immediately were "Chinese accents" and "communication barriers". Chinese in America, especially those who came in the 80's and 90's, speak English with strong Chinese accents. They struggled with communication at work place due to the language barrier. So I put these two down on my list. As Chinese myself, I was anxious to learn what stereotypes my American colleagues came up with. After we all finished jotting down the stereotypes about each ethnic group, the instructor posted the four ethnic groups on the wall in different sections. We then went to each section to add our stereotypes. We only wrote unique ones. We each had twenty colored dots. After the stereotypes were all written on the paper on the wall, we put our dots on those we thought were more popular. My eyes were naturally riveted on the list for Chinese.

Much to my surprise, the following stereotypes about Chinese came on top: Bruce Lee, Jackie Chen, Kong Fu, TaiChi, mathematicians, hardworking, smart, anti-social, rude, loud, and manners, to name a few. The two expressions I contributed did not even make to the popular list. Bruce Lee and Jackie Chen are both successful Hollywood movies stars for their stunning Kong Fu performances. Association of Chinese with Bruce Lee or Jackie Chen implies that Chinese are perceived to have Kung Fu. TaiChi is indeed popular in China, but most of the overseas Chinese in America do not practice TaiChi. Chinese education system puts heavy emphasis on foundational skills training. Math is one of the key subjects rigorously taught at Chinese schools. Many Chinese students, however, have math phobia, too. They have no choice but go through the rigorous training. We are taught that China is a nation of hardworking people. Chinese students often outperform their classmates in tests. It is no surprise that they are considered to be smart. On the other hand, Chinese are associated with negative stereotypes such as anti-social, rude, loud and lack of manners. Out of curiosity, I asked my colleagues how they formed the negative stereotypes about Chinese. Was it because they encountered some Chinese who were rude to them? Not to offend me, they unanimously told me that they heard the stories from their friends. Regardless, Americans have stereotypes about Chinese. Some are positive but others are negative. Positive or negative, stereotypes are stereotypes. They are barriers to fair and respectful treatment of human beings. Each individual is different in his or her own way. As such, they should be respected and treated as individuals. One's success should be measured based one's performance but not on a stereotype. When I ask for a calculator, I have the need to use one. It does not matter whether others need one or not.

24 TO ACCEPT OR DECLINE THE CLOCK

Three days after my family moved into the house we had bought, Bob, our realtor, came to visit us. Bob is an experienced realtor. I came to know him while searching for a house. He used to be an engineer, but continued to work as a realtor after retirement. As our buyer's agent, he did a fantastic job of finding what we wanted.

As expected, Bob arrived at 10:00am in the morning, carrying with him a gift bag. My wife greeted him at the door when she heard the doorbell ring.

"How do you like your new house?" he inquired, curious to know whether we liked the house he helped us find

"I like it very much," answered my wife, beaming with smiles. "It's my dream house. Thank you so much for finding us the house." My wife was indeed grateful to Bob. .As a realtor, it is a challenge to find a house your prospective buyer likes in terms of location, price, and style. Bob was relieved to be able to find one for us. After all, we had been searching for more than 6 months without luck.

"That's fantastic!" Bob was glad that we liked the house. "It's indeed a nice one. You got a good deal."

The sales price included 3.5% commission for Bob, but we were willing to pay the commission. It was not easy to find a house to your liking without using an agent, especially in those days when listing of houses for sale was not accessible to the general public.

My wife led Bob to the spacious family room, which was not decorated yet except a sofa and a love seat.

"Have a seat on the sofa, please," my wife said to Bob. She was being super sweet, still immersed in the joy of having purchased her dream house.

"Thank you!" Bob sat down, leaving the bag on the floor. He was clearly in jubilant mood, too. We were the second client he had helped in a month. He was very satisfied with what he had accomplished in a month. For him, the more houses he helped buy or sell, the more money he would make.

"Do you feel like a cup of tea?" I offered Bob, trying to show my hospitality to him. "It is a famous tea in China, called Long Jing." Americans typically drink tea in tea bags such as Lipton brands. Not many make tea with loose tea leaves as we Chinese do.

"Sure, I will try." Bob was happy to accept the offer. "I never tried loose leaves before, but trust your recommendation."

While I was boiling water, Bob stood up and said to my wife and me, "Mrs. and Mr. Lin, I brought you a clock as a house warming gift to you. Hope you like it." With that, Bob handed the bag over to my wife.

My brain froze momentarily at the mere mention of "gift clock", not knowing how to respond. My wife, however, was quick to respond.

"Not necessary, Bob," my wife told Bob. "We have plenty of clocks at home. No need to spend money on this. You can give it to your next client. It's very considerate of you to bring a gift to us. We very much appreciate your kindness." My wife attempted to decline the gift as politely as she could. I knew why she wanted to decline the gift. I would have done the same. With high emotional intelligence, she knew how not to hurt others' feelings. I truly admired her for that.

"Well, I have given a clock to every client I have helped to buy a house. It has been my way of thanking my clients for the business and the trust they placed in me. Some even referred their friends to me. As a realtor, you have to build a relationship with clients. Closing a deal is not the end of the story. You have to make friends with them. That's how you grow your business." Bob tried to talk us into accepting the gift and explained to us that the clock was meant to further our friendship. His point was that our business relationship ended but our friendship started. The continued friendship would help him get more clients in the future. For realtors, reputation is gold. Word of mouth may be more effective in generating sales than advertisements.

"Just curious, have you helped a Chinese client before?" my wife asked.

"No. You are the first Chinese client I have helped," Bob answered, looking a bit bewildered by my wife's question. He probably wondered why Chinese had anything to do with his gift. He started to have a hunch that there was something about the gift that made us hesitant to accept.

"This Seiko desk clock is just a normal gift. There is nothing special about it. It's my token of appreciation to you," Bob said, hoping that we would accept the gift. He probably had not been involved in a dilemma like this before. Who would not accept a gift?

"Bob, I know it's hard for you to understand the Chinese gift culture," I said to Bob, thinking that it would not help if we continued to beat about the bush. We had to let him know the reason about our hesitation to accept the gift clock. The confused look on our face sent a message to Bob. He started to realize that the gift was not appropriate.

"So, please be frank with me. Did I offend you with the gift?" Bob wanted to know the reason badly. What started out as a warm welcome now turned into an awkward silence. We were all embarrassed by the unexpected situation we found ourselves in.

My wife and I looked at each other, each signaling the other to answer Bob's question. After a moment of hesitation, I mustered courage to tell Bob the truth.

"Bob, it is hard to explain, but in the Chinese gift culture, clocks are not recommended as gifts," I explained, still hedging on my choice of words.

"Why?" Bob got really curious about my incomplete explanation.

"In Chinese, the English word 'clock' is pronounced as 'zhong' in Chinese, which happens to be the same pronunciation as another character, which means 'end of life'. When you send a clock to somebody, you are sending 'end of life' (song zhong) to that person. Literally, 'song zhong' means saying goodbye to a dead person." As I explained, I noticed a subtle change in Bob's confused look. He seemed to have got it.

"Now I understand. I'm terribly sorry about this. I never knew the cultural difference. Excuse my ignorance and innocence. I really did not mean to make you feel bad about this gift." Realizing why we were hesitant to accept his gift, Bob apologized sincerely to us.

"Well, no need to feel bad," I comforted Bob. "It's not your fault. We may not know similar taboos in American culture."

"I will return the clock to the store and get you a different gift," Bob said.

Surprisingly, the moment we cleared the confusion, I was tremendously relieved. I was no longer concerned about the clock taboo. After all, it was called "clock" in English. As long as we use English, we would be fine.

"Well, if we say it in English, it is 'clock'. So what is bad in China may not be so in America. I do not want you to have the trouble of returning the clock. We can accept the clock." I reassured Bob.

"Are you sure?" Bob asked, a bit surprised by the sudden change in my attitude.

"Yep, clocks are clocks. As the English saying goes, when in Rome do as the Romans do. Now that we are in America, let's do as American do." For some reason, I found it silly to let the Chinese pronunciation create the emotional stress both to Bob and us. My wife neither agreed nor disagreed with me. She had reservation about what I said. Not that I did not care about cultural differences, but that I felt guilty of putting Bob through the painful dilemma. I just could not imagine Bob returning the clock and getting us a different gift. Instead of forcing Bob to adapt to the Chinese culture, we could adapt to the American culture. The solution to the dilemma was simple: we say the clock in English only. What a relief!

With Bob recovering from the emotional stress we imposed on him, I made him a cup of Long Jing tea. He loved it. As he was enjoying the tea, he became increasingly relaxed. He shared with us his stories as a realtor. Fifteen minutes later, he had to leave and meet with another prospective buyer.

After Bob left, my wife and I decided to put the clock away for the time being. Because we just bought a new house, we expected our Chinese friends would come to visit us in the next few weeks. Out of sight, and out of mind. We did not want this to bother us. We did not want our friends to know that the clock was a gift to us.

25 HANDS UP!

It was a gloomy, windy, late summer day. I accompanied my friend to shop for a used car. He and I car pooled for a few months when his car broke down. The engine was burnt due to the oil being too thick and dirty. I asked why he had not done oil change for his car. He explained that he used to drive the car locally a few miles a day, so he would only do the oil change every six months. Now that he had car pooled with me, and we each drove our own car on alternate days, he easily added more than 3,000 miles to the car. Plus he had already driven the car for more than 3 months before we car pooled. As a general rule, you are told to do oil change every three months or 3,000 miles whichever comes first. So, my friend learned the lesson the hard way. It was also a costly lesson. The old car could have been traded in for at least a few thousand dollars.

Having lost a car by his own negligence, my friend was in a hurry to purchase a used one. In America, without a car is like without legs. You cannot go anywhere. You may do without a car if you live in a big city such as Chicago or New York, where public transportation is available. In most residential towns or cities, car is the only option available to you. Since we were carpooling, I was motivated to drive him around to find a car he wanted. Otherwise, I would have to drive every day. Commuting to work is not bad if you have somebody with you talking and chatting about odds and ends or events or things that happen around you or at work. I would prefer to sit in the passenger seat, though. High concentration during driving makes you exhausted easily. So, I was in a way also anxious to help him find a car.

After visiting a couple of dealers, we found one at Clark, a local dealer in Hudson, Ohio. The sales guy did a fantastic job of selling it to my friend.

Before closing the deal, my friend wanted to test drive the car, as is a common practice by customers. He got into the driver's seat and I got into the passenger's seat. Looking around inside the car, he was pleased. It was a 5-year old Toyota Camry with 6,000 miles. It was in excellent condition. Apparently, the previous owner took good care of the car.

He carefully drove his way out of the crowded parking lot and onto the local highway Terex Road.

"How do you like it?" I asked.

"I like it a lot," he answered gleefully, not able to hide his satisfaction. "The engine runs very quietly. The acceleration is quick."

"Well, to truly test acceleration, you need to slow down and push the gas pedal hard to see how fast it picks up speed," I suggested, as if I were an expert mechanic.

"That's a good idea," he concurred.

He slowed the car down to 25 miles per hour, and then pushed the gas pedal hard. Off went the car, roaring and leaving smoke behind the car. The acceleration was fast and impressive.

Just as I was going to make positive comments about the car, I heard a siren sounding 100 feet away from us. The flashing blue, red and white lights on top of a police car caught us off guard.

"Stop! There is a cop over there," I warned my friend.

He applied the brake quickly, and the car stopped with a grinding noise, leaving tire prints on the road. We could smell rubber burning. I asked him to pull the car to the side of the road. Panic-stricken, he asked me what to do. I knew we were in trouble. A speeding ticket was coming his way for sure. He would have to pay the fine, which is proportional to the miles above the speed limit. The speed limit for the road was 45 miles. The car accelerated close to 55 miles. Based on past experience, the fine would be at least $100.

It was simply a bad day! We did not realize the acceleration would give rise to speeding. Much less did we expect a police officer was ambushing nearby on the road.

My friend was getting increasingly nervous as we saw the police officer approaching our car.

"Jason, can you go and explain to the police officer what we were doing?" he asked.

I knew it would be hard for him to explain it to the police officer because he was verbally challenged due to his inadequate English skill, so I agreed to try. I got out of the car from the passenger door and walked towards the police officer with anxiety.

The moment I started walking to the police officer, he shouted, "Don't move! Put your hands up and lean against the car!" The police officer pulled out his gun quickly, pointing at me directly.

The police officer's order was loud enough to wake the dead, sending a chill down my spine. Never before had I been ordered by a police officer to hold my hands up. I felt humiliated as if I was a criminal getting arrested—a scene I often see in a Hollywood movie. On the other hand, I was helpless. I heard the police officer's order loud and clear. So, I obeyed his order. Any attempt from my end to disobey the order could lead to deadly consequences. Plus, at worst, it was merely a traffic violation. It was not a criminal offense. So, I did not think the police officer would handcuff me as long as I held my hands up as he ordered.

When the police officer approached the car, he asked my friend to show his driver's license. After checking the driver's license, the police officer asked for proof of car insurance. By Ohio law, drivers must have car insurance. Luckily, my friend had his insurance card with him. The police officer validated the insurance card carefully. The atmosphere started to change. He looked less intimidating now.

"May I put down my hands now?" I asked nervously.

"Yes," he answered, sounding much friendlier now.

"Sir, we were test driving the car to see its acceleration. Sorry we did not realize that we were speeding." I was explaining the incident to the police officer in a bid to avoid a speeding ticket.

For some reason, the police officer was not in the mood to issue a speeding ticket to my friend. Instead, he issued a courtesy warning, which incurred no fine. Otherwise, a speeding ticket could cost more than $100.

"Thank you very much!" my friend and I said unanimously when we saw the warning note.

The police officer went back to his car, possibly to continue his ambush there. My friend's mood was totally ruined. He did not want to test drive the car any more.

"Let's go back now. I'm fine with the car." With that, he drove back to the dealer.

He made the payment, and drove the car home. The experience bothered me. I told the sales guy the incident we had just encountered.

"When you are stopped by a cop," he explained. "You should stop the car in a safe place as quickly as possible. Turn off the car, turn on the internal light, open the window part way and place your hands on the wheel. If you get out of the car, and reach your hand into your pocket, the cop may think you are reaching out for a gun... You know what I mean?"

Before he continued, I got the point. "Thank you. Now I understand why the police officer ordered me to have my hands up."

On the way home, I no longer felt humiliated. The police officer did what he was trained to do. I learned the lesson the hard way. Do not get out of the car when you are stopped by a police officer.

26 A NEIGHBOR IN NEED IS A NEIGHBOR INDEED

After 12 years of reliable service, the refrigerator in our house started to show signs of aging. It had to be replaced. My wife and I shopped around and found one we both liked without much trouble. It was a modern, slick-looking Samsung.

When the delivery truck brought the new refrigerator to our house, we were excited to welcome the new appliance home. It had more features, and more storage space. It was more energy efficient and much better than the old one. The stainless chassis added modern look to the kitchen. The upgrade was worth the money. However, our excitement was soon dampened. The new one was bigger than the old one. It was too wide to pass through the space between the kitchen wall and the counter top in the kitchen. The delivery man gave us two options: either keep the refrigerator or have it taken back to the store and get a smaller one. It was summer time. I had to get a refrigerator that day because my old one broke. Food would go bad unless we got a new one that day. Moreover, my wife and I really liked the new one, which was modern and to our liking. I asked the delivery man if he and his co-worker could move the refrigerator over the counter into the kitchen. They politely rejected my request. Their company policy would not allow them to do anything not in line with the company policy. Lifting the heavy refrigerator over the counter could injure their backs. What if in doing so, they damaged the refrigerator or something in the kitchen? It was understandable that they did not want to take chances.

It was indeed a tough problem to solve. I scratched my head for a solution but was not able to come up with a feasible one.

"How about getting a smaller one instead?" I consulted with my wife. As you know, women have the final say, especially when it comes to decisions on home décor or home remodeling projects.

"Are you crazy? This is the one we all like. I would rather cut the countertop than settle down on a smaller one." She was adamant about getting the big one. Once she made up her mind, it would not be easy to change her mind unless the change was a better option.

"Well, the delivery guys won't move the big one over the countertop into the kitchen. If we want to keep the big one, we cannot leave it here without moving it into the kitchen. So, the only option left is to cut the countertop by a couple of inches to widen the passage into the kitchen." I tried to rationalize our decision with my wife.

Cutting the countertop would not be too bad. A table saw would do the job. It would be quite a project to fix it up. To cut or not to cut, that was a question.

"Go ahead and do it," my wife was determined to get the big one into the kitchen. She did not seem to be joking.

I went to the basement and got the table saw up. "Am I crazy?" I thought to myself. "Is it worth the trouble cutting the countertop to move the big refrigerator into the kitchen? How to repair the cut? Will the countertop look weird after it's shortened by a couple of inches?" The more I thought about the cut, the less comfortable I felt about the decision. It appeared to be more irrational to me. It reminded me of the Chinese idiom of "cutting your toes to fit in the shoes". This could be a laughing stock to our friends.

"Are you sure you want to cut the countertop?" I asked my wife again.

"I don't know," she answered with hesitation. She no longer sounded as firm now. The image of shortening the countertop made her think twice.

"It's your decision, but we are NOT responsible for any damage to the countertop if you guys decide to cut it," the delivery man cautioned us. He was clearly not in favor of cutting the countertop. Moreover, he and his co-worker would have to wait much longer to complete the delivery. In their business, they did not like exceptions. They would avoid trouble as much as they could.

My wife and I looked at each other. Our eye contact suggested the same thing: it would not be wise to cut the countertop to move the refrigerator. We both seemed to have thought about the Chinese idiom. It was not

"Great minds think alike", but husband and wife do have a special wave length for communication. Once they hit the wave length, they understand each other perfectly. So, in the end, our sobriety overcame our eagerness to get the new refrigerator. We decided to return the bulky one to the store and get a smaller one instead.

As the delivery men started to move the bulky one out of the house, I stayed on the driveway, watching them with frustration and disappointment.

"What's up, Jason?" Shawn asked me, driving his pick-up truck onto his driveway. Shawn was my new next door neighbor.

"Well, I bought a new refrigerator, but it was too big and the delivery guys could not get it into the kitchen," I replied, sounding helpless and in despair.

"If you don't mind, I can take a look," Shawn offered to help me out, much to my surprise.

"Oh, please," I pleaded with him. "If you can solve the problem, I will really appreciate it."

Shawn's offer re-kindled my hope. After inspecting the refrigerator carefully, he went to our kitchen and looked around. "Well, the only way you can move the bulky refrigerator in is to lift it over the counter," Shawn suggested, sounding professional and confident.

"Yes," I concurred, thinking Shaw's suggestion was logical.

"But the delivery guys would not do it because of the company policy," I explained.

"Yea, I understand. I can ask John, who works for me, to help me, and we two should be able to get the monster into your kitchen. How does that sound to you?" Shawn was ready to execute his plan.

Meanwhile, my wife caught my conversation with Shawn and rushed out to the driveway. "Really?" she was still doubtful, but her eyes lit up right away.

"Yes," Shawn affirmed with professional confidence.

"That's wonderful! " My wife could not conceal her excitement about the prospect of owning the new refrigerator. Her dream moved a step closer to reality.

So, I signed the delivery paper and accepted the refrigerator, trusting that Shawn would make the day for us. The delivery men moved the old one out of the house. Their mission was accomplished.

Shawn brought John with him, a big Dolly, and a couple of blankets. He covered the countertop with the blankets. Each wrapped his waist with a protection belt. At the sight of their professional moving equipment, and the preparation work they did, I knew they were going to succeed. The doubt I had before quickly dissipated. After moving the monster with the Dolly to the counter, Shawn and John lifted it over the countertop and carefully moved it down into the kitchen area. Shawn and John looked strong and their arms were muscular like those of a body builder. I was amazed to see them move the monster with no additional help. They were clearly skilled in moving.

Once the monster was in the kitchen, Shawn offered to help me install the refrigerator. I could not thank him enough and happily accepted his offer. Shawn glanced through the install instructions, and knew exactly what to do. Within ten minutes, he connected the water supply line and moved the refrigerator into position. He turned on the refrigerator and inspected it professionally, making sure it functioned as expected. Shawn went above and beyond my expectation. I truly appreciated his help and admired him for his muscle, knowledge and skill. My wife of course couldn't be happier.

"How come you are so confident about moving the monster into the kitchen?" I was curious about Shawn's skill.

"I own a moving company. We are used to moving big items."

"No wonder," I said. "I am glad that I have a neighbor in the business of moving house."

"Let me know if you need us," Shawn said, relieved to have accomplished something that was a big deal to us.

I paid Shawn $200 for his service. Shawn was very happy to receive the money because it was more than he had expected. Plus it was a business opportunity he had not anticipated. If he had not seen me on the driveway, we would have settled for a smaller unit. My family would not be as happy. A neighbor in need is a neighbor indeed.

ABOUT THE AUTHOR

Jason Lin claims to be a "professional" student. He studied Engineering in Nanking, and later English Language in Suzhou, and finally got his mater in English from Shanghai International Studies University. He pursued an advanced degree in Rhetoric and Linguistics in America, but ended up with MBA with concentration on MIS. Instead of pursuing a management career, his passion about engineering "flared up" and motivated him to pursue an advanced degree in Computer Science. He finally realized that he was also a husband and father. Being a professional student, he could not raise his family. So he found a job while working on his Ph. D program. Since then, he has been in IT management for more than 20 years.

He is the Vice Chair of Chinese Cultural Garden Association in Cleveland, Ohio. He served as Chair of Asian American Network of a Fortune 100 company. He has been a successful IT leader. As President of Linguasoft International Ltd, he has dedicated time and resources to provide free online education to kids through www.pointsforkids.com.

Jason Lin was a well published researcher in China. He also published a research paper in ACM, a prestigious journal in America while pursuing his Ph. D. However, Jason Lin found more gratification in writing stories and essays instead of research papers.